# ONE, TWO, WHAT DID DADDY DO?

ALSO BY SUSAN ROGERS COOPER

*Chasing Away the Devil*
*Other People's Houses*
*Houston in the Rear View Mirror*
*The Man in the Green Chevy*

# ONE, TWO, WHAT DID DADDY DO?

## Susan Rogers Cooper

ST. MARTIN'S PRESS
New York

Design by Judith Christensen

Library of Congress Cataloging-in-Publication Data

Cooper, Susan Rogers.
    One, two, what did daddy do? / Susan Rogers Cooper.
      p.  cm.
    "A Thomas Dunne book."
    ISBN 0-312-08209-6 (hardcover)
    I. Title.
  PS3553.O623505  1992
    813'.54—dc20                              92-26160
                                                      CIP

First Edition: November 1992

10 9 8 7 6 5 4 3 2 1

I would like to acknowledge the invaluable assistance of Don Cooper, whose original concept the characters of E.J. and Willis Pugh were, and Evin Cooper, who, at the age of twelve, managed to plot most of the book. I would like to take this opportunity to thank them for allowing me to type it all up.

I would also like to thank the following writers for their input and support during the project: Cindy Bonner, Barbara Burnett Smith, Mary Willis Walker, Dinah Chenven, Susan Wade, and Sally Ples. A special thank-you to mystery writer Jan Grape for her generosity in sharing her expertise.

No acknowledgment would be complete without a heartfelt thanks to my editor, Ruth Cavin, and my agent, Anita Diamant, both of whom have supported and encouraged me on this and every other project.

—Susan Rogers Cooper
September 24, 1991

FOR MY PARENTS,
GEORGE AND EDYTHE ROGERS,
FOR THEIR LOVE AND
SUPPORT

# 1

I threw myself spread-eagle across the doorway. "No," I said.

"E.J.," he said. He looked at me. "Come on."

"You can't leave me alone with them."

Willis sighed. "It won't be long. They'll be gone in just a little while." He looked at his watch. "I've got a meeting in twenty minutes."

"Bullshit," I said, standing my ground.

That's when we heard them. Thundering down the stairs. Screams of "Did so!" and "Did not!" wafting our way. Then there was the sound of a thud, a wail, and our four-year-old daughter fell into the kitchen, holding onto her arm and screaming. "He hit me!"

"Did not!" came from the doorway where our seven-year-old son stood, looking superior.

I left my perch by the back door and went to Megan, picking her up and checking her arm. I heard the door open and turned to see Willis scrambling through the opening with a quick "See ya!" over his shoulder.

"Coward!" I yelled after him. "Turncoat! Traitor!" Checking my daughter, I found no blood or anything resembling the beginnings of a bruise.

Graham marched into the room. "I didn't hit her," he said. "She tripped."

I glowered, Megan glared, and I started breakfast. The quick one. Cereal, milk, OJ, and toast. Looking at my daughter again, I said, "Megan, your pants are on wrong-side out."

Graham glanced at his sister and began to laugh. "Geek! Nerd!"

Four-year-old Megan looked at her brother and said, "Asshole!"

"Megan! We don't talk like that in this house!" I said, pulling down her blue jeans and turning them right-side out.

"Daddy does," she replied, looking at me with those big blue eyes.

It had rained that weekend. Howling, torrential downpours that lasted the entire weekend. The kind of Texas weather that songs are written about. Lightning, thunder, flash-flood warnings, tornado alerts—you name it, we got it. Ah, spring. Nothing stood between Willis and me and the wrath of our children but a much used and much seen videocassette of *The Little Mermaid*.

All I could think of was that, once breakfast was out of the way, I'd have them in the car, along with my neighbor's kids, drive them to two different schools, then have four blessed hours to myself. The thought alone was orgasmic.

That Monday morning in April was my day to drive the kids. My friend Terry and I traded off weeks. It was convenient, since Terry and Roy lived right next door. Our driveways even connected. The car pool was only for the younger kids: my Megan, aged four and seven-year-old Graham, plus Terry's ten-year-old, Aldon, and her

2

four-year-old, Megan's best friend, Bessie. Terry's oldest daughter, Monique, sixteen, usually grabbed a ride with her father, since the high school started earlier.

I herded the kids to the car, Graham grabbing blossoms off my rain-and-hail-trampled azalea bushes to stick down his sister's T-shirt.

"Stop that and get in the car!" I said.

"She started it!"

"Did not!"

"Did so!"

I grabbed Graham by the arm and gently tossed him into the back seat. "Shut up! Fasten your seat belt!"

"I'm calling the child abuse hotline!"

"Fine. A few days in jail would be preferable to putting up with you. Now shut up." I fastened Megan into her seat belt, grabbing at her hands as she tried to pelt her brother with the seat belt's wicked end. Finally, I got behind the wheel and started the car, tapping gently on the horn for Terry. After about two minutes, I hit the horn again, not so gently. It was the third time that month I'd had to wait for the Lester kids and I wasn't in the mood. I turned off the ignition and got out of the car. Looking in the back seat, I noticed Graham reaching for his seat belt.

"You unbuckle that thing and I'll knock you unconscious."

"Yeah, you and what army?"

"Watch your sister."

"Why? Is she gonna do tricks?"

I gave them both my "I'm the mistress of the universe—you fuck with me, you die" look and said, "Stay. Don't move. Not a muscle. Not an eyelash! I'll be right back." I turned, took two steps, stopped, and with my back still to them, said, "I said don't move!" Thus, in my small way, perpetuating the legend of mothers with eyes in the backs of their heads.

3

I walked quickly to Terry's back door and rapped on the glass, then opened the door and stuck my head in.

"Terry! Ya'll ready?"

There was no answer. The only light in the kitchen was the one over the stove top, the one I knew Terry used as a night light. There were no boxes of corn flakes and Froot Loops on the table. No milk spilled on the floor. And, omen of omens, no coffee in the automatic coffeemaker. I said, "Shit," rather loudly, knowing my friend and her family had overslept, and started through the kitchen into the dining room. From there I crossed the foyer, turned right, and headed for the stairs.

That's when I saw it. I wasn't sure at first what the mess was. Just dark smears on the landing walls. I flipped the switch at the bottom of the stairs and a light shone down on stairs and landing. Then the smell hit me. That sweet, cloying smell. Leaving the light on, I backed down the foyer, staring at the mess on the walls. I'm not sure when my mind actually formed the word "blood," but when it did, I turned and hightailed it out of the house.

At that point my mind was mostly blank. At least I remember it that way. There were two things I knew had to be done. Get my children into their own home and call somebody. Anybody.

The kids were out of their seatbelts, Megan in the front seat throwing the quarters I keep in the ashtray at her brother, who had somehow made it into the cargo area of the station wagon. I opened the front door and pulled Megan out.

"Graham did it!" she wailed.

"Did not!" came from the cargo area.

I opened the tailgate. "Out!"

He stood his ground. "I didn't do nothin'! Megan started it!"

I had Megan half off the ground with my hold on her

4

upper arm. Reaching inside the cargo area, I grabbed Graham's ankle and began to pull.

"Gawd, Mom! I didn't do nothin'!"

"Get out now!" I yelled. Looking at me for the first time, maybe in his entire life, Graham stopped for a full second, frowned into my face, then scurried out. "In the house now. Take your sister."

"But . . ." he started, thought better of it and ran for the front door, dragging a screaming Megan with him. I beat them there, my keys in my hand, and unlocked the door.

"Go upstairs!" I said, heading for the phone.

"But . . ."

"Get up the goddamn stairs!"

They ran up the stairs, Megan no longer having to be pulled, more than happy to get as far away from her crazy mother as possible.

I picked up the phone and dialed 911.

"Codderville Emergency Services."

"Ah . . . this is E. J. Pugh . . . in Black Cat Ridge. Something's wrong . . ."

"Ma'am?"

I took a deep breath, but it seemed to stick somewhere around my breastbone. "There's something wrong at . . ." All of a sudden I couldn't remember Terry's address. I knew it was two numbers less than mine, but I couldn't remember mine either. "On Sagebrush Trail in Black Cat Ridge. Number . . . 1411. That's it. Fourteen eleven! My neighbors . . . there's blood on the walls . . ."

"Where are you calling from, ma'am?"

"My house. Fourteen-thirteen. Sagebrush Trail."

"What's the cross street, ma'am?"

"Cross street? Oh, ah . . . Morning Glory Lane. Off Black Cat Boulevard."

"I've dispatched an officer, ma'am. He should be there in a moment. Meanwhile, I'd like you to stay on the line with me, okay?"

"Yeah. Okay. I don't know what's happening. I went over there because the kids didn't come out to the car . . ."

"Ma'am?"

"We carpool . . . and the kids didn't come out. So I went over there. When I went in . . ."

"The door was unlocked, ma'am?"

"Yes . . . we don't lock up much around here . . ." Saying it made me turn and look at my own door, not even latched, still standing open from my mad rush into the house. Stretching the cord as far as it would reach, I pushed in the locking mechanism and slammed the door shut.

"The officer should be there shortly, ma'am."

"Okay. I can't imagine . . . maybe they're hurt . . . maybe you should send an ambulance . . ."

"The officer will notify us if that's necessary, ma'am."

"Oh . . ."

There was a presence on the staircase. I could feel it. I looked up to see Megan looking down at me, tears streaming down her cheeks, her pretty face scrunched up in her mad look.

"Hold on a moment, please," I said to the 911 operator. Putting my hand over the mouthpiece, I said to my daughter, "Megan . . ."

"I'm not speaking to Bessie no more . . ."

"Anymore . . ."

She hiccuped. "Anymore, ever, never."

"Honey, I'm on the phone . . ."

"She won't even say hi."

"Go back upstairs . . ." I stopped and dropped the phone. "Bessie?" I asked. "Megan, where is she?"

"Standing at her window. Being mean!"

I headed up the stairs two at a time. "Show me, honey. Show me where she is."

Taking my hand, Megan led me to her room, which looked out at Terry's house next door. Megan's and Bes-

6

sie's rooms faced each other, and Terry and I had been talking about stringing a line between the two rooms so the girls could send each other notes. When and if they ever learned to write. I ran to the window and pulled back the Strawberry Shortcake curtains. There, across the way, stood Bessie, staring out a second story window, her hair and face matted with rusty red.

I scooped Megan up in the my arms and ran with her into Graham's bedroom. "Keep your sister in here!"

"Mom!"

"Do it!"

I ran down the stairs, forgetting about the phone trailing on the floor.

The back door of the Lesters' house was still open, just the way I left it. And somewhere upstairs, beyond the blood, Bessie stood, obviously hurt but alive. I knew I couldn't wait for the police, or the ambulance, or anyone else. I was there. And so was Bessie.

I've never thought to ask myself if I'm brave. That's not one of those characteristics women think a lot about. That's a man's bailiwick. In retrospect, I don't think going after Bessie was all that brave, not if bravery is a conscious decision. I was running on instinct; there was nothing conscious about going into that house at all.

Once inside, I followed the trail I had taken earlier, through the kitchen, the dining room, right at the foyer to the stairs. The stairwell light was still on, as I'd left it, shining down on the reddish brown muck on the walls. Ignoring the sight and the smell, I hurried up the stairs to the landing and, turning, started to head up the second half of the flight but tripped, falling face first. And landing on ten-year-old Aldon, lying on his back, his eyes opened, the formerly feisty blue eyes now almost opaque in death. The top of his pajamas was covered in blood. I scrambled off him, throwing myself backwards against the wall. I felt the bile rise in my throat and, jumping to my feet, ran back down the stairs for the clear air outside. I gulped in lungfuls of warm spring air. My body was shaking all over and I knew I had to get home, back to my own babies and away from whatever happened at the Lester house. After two steps in the direction of my own home, I remembered Bessie. Standing at the window. Staring into space. Covered with blood and gore. But alive. I couldn't leave four-year-old Bessie in the house. I couldn't.

I hugged the wall as I stepped gingerly around little Aldon, trying not to touch or disturb him in any way. At the head of the stairs I turned right again, starting toward the end of the hall where Bessie's room was. Terry and Roy's room was the first on the left. My eyes seemed to have a mind of their own and swiveled to the open doorway of the parents' room.

Sitting on the floor, his back against the open door, was Roy, or what was left of him. I only recognized him from the pajamas I'd helped Terry pick out last Christmas. Royal blue Chinese silk. They'd cost $150. Between the legs of royal blue silk rested a shotgun, Roy's fingers still on the trigger guard, though the muzzle had dropped across his left arm. His face was gone. The cheesy little mustache he could never grow right blown away. The cockeyed blue eyes that Terry insisted were sexier than Paul Newman's, the crooked incisor that gave his smile that little-boy quality. All gone. Maybe they were somewhere on the floor, but I didn't think they'd do Roy any good any more.

I gripped the doorjamb to steady myself. When I moved my hand to continue on down the hall, I saw the bloody handprint. My own. I looked down at my hands and the front of my shirt, all covered with blood. Aldon's blood, no doubt. At some point, I heard a high keening sound. It took just a moment before I realized it was coming from me.

8

I found a focal point high on the wall, one of several blue rosebuds bordering the ceiling. I focused and began the breathing I'd learned at Lamaze class. Deep cleansing breath to begin. Breathe out two short, one long. Three times. Deep cleansing breath to end. I steadied myself and continued down the hall.

The first room on the left was Monique's. My babysitter. The girl who trusted me with her heart's secrets. The door was open. Monique was in a sitting position against the back wall, her eyes squinched shut, her mouth in a grimace. Blood from her body spattered the wall behind her, leaving a red Rorschach pattern on the posters of M.C. Hammer and Jon Bon Jovi. Terry lay across Monique's bed, the back of her nightgown covered in blood.

I moved to Terry's body and gingerly picked up her hand, feeling for a pulse I knew wasn't there. I sobbed out loud. "Christ!" One eye was hidden by the blanket. The other stared dully at me. I touched the lid softly, pulling it down to close over the big, cocker spaniel brown eye. I wanted to stay there forever. Just hold her in my arms and cry. But I didn't. Turning, I quickly moved across the hall to Bessie's room.

She still stood where I had seen her from Megan's window. Staring ahead of her into space, her little arms by her sides, her back to me. She looked so angelic standing there. Her pretty little pink nightgown, her long dark brown hair falling in tresses down her back.

I gulped in air, steadied myself against the doorjamb and said, "Bessie? Honey, it's me, Auntie E.J."

There was no movement from the window. "Bessie, honey, we're going to go to my house and play with Megan, okay? You want to do that?"

I moved cautiously towards her and gently turned her to face me. Her eyes, carbon copies of her mother's, didn't track. They moved where her body moved, but they weren't seeing anything. From the back she had seemed angelically aloof from all the mess around her, but turning her I saw the front: the blood-matted night-dress, clumps of something foul on her face and in her hair. I picked her up in my arms. "We're going to go play with Megan now," I cooed. "Just you and me. How does that sound?"

I pressed her face against my breast as I made the long journey back down the hall, down the stairs, and out of the house.

# 2

One of Codderville's finest found me puking in the oleander bushes that separated Terry's yard from mine. Bessie was standing silently beside me, staring off into space.

"Mrs. Pugh?" he called, rapidly exiting his cruiser.

I pointed back towards Terry's house and said, "They're all *d-e-a-d*."

"Ma'am?"

I rolled over from my all-fours position into sitting.

"Ma'am, are you hurt?" he asked.

"No, but *she* is!"

The officer squatted next to me and pulled Bessie gently to him. She came docilely. Together we checked her out for cuts or shotgun wounds. We found none.

"What's wrong with her?" I said, my voice dangerously close to a whine.

The officer stood up and headed for his car. "I don't know, ma'am. I'm not a doctor—maybe shock." He shrugged. "I'm calling an ambulance and some backup now."

He made his call and came back, his hand on the butt of his gun riding low on his hip.

"Aren't you going to go in there?" I screeched. I really did. It was beginning to hit me. I wanted someone to *do* something, and he was the only someone within yelling range.

"Ma'am, just sit quietly until the ambulance arrives, please."

"They're all d-e-a-d in there! And you're not doing a goddamned thing about it!" I stood up, my face within inches of his.

He put his hands on my arms and gently pushed me out of his space. "Ma'am, just sit down there on the lawn with the little girl. We'll take a look at the house as soon as my backup arrives."

"Backup!" I snorted. "Jesus, they're dead, they're not going to hurt you!"

Remembering Bessie, I sat back down on the lawn and pulled her into my lap, stroking her matted hair away from her face. "It's okay, baby, everything's going to be okay." It was then that I started crying.

I don't know how long it took the ambulance and the other police to show up. Time seemed to have stopped and sped up and slowed down, all at the same time. When the EMTs got there, they checked Bessie over, finding what the cop and I had found: nothing. No cuts, no bruises, no abrasions, nothing.

When they started loading her onto the stretcher for the ambulance, I found the first officer and said, "I've got to go with her."

"Okay, ma'am."

"But my kids are alone in my house . . ."

"Becks!" he called, motioning toward a woman in uniform standing around with every other Codderville cop on the force.

She sauntered towards us, her hands resting on her Sam Browne belt riding low on her hips.

"Yeah, Jimmy?"

"Mrs. Pugh here needs to go to the hospital with the little girl, but her kids are alone in her house over there." He pointed. "You wanna baby-sit?"

She shrugged. "Beats standing around with my thumb up my ass."

My kids were in for a treat. A real role model. "Could you call my husband?"

The first cop, Jimmy, gave me a slip of paper and a pen and I wrote down Willis' number at work and handed it to Becks. Then I crawled into the back of the ambulance with Bessie. A plainclothes cop crawled in with me.

Holding out his hand, he said, "I'm Detective Stewart, Mrs. Pugh. Mind if I ride with you and get your statement?"

I looked at Bessie, then at one of the EMTs working on her. "Can she understand me?" I asked.

He shook his head. "I don't know, ma'am. I don't think so. I think she's in shock."

I moved to the back of the ambulance and Detective Stewart followed. There I told him everything, from the moment I first walked into the house until I came out and puked in the oleanders. By the time I'd finished, we'd arrived at the emergency-room entrance to Codderville Memorial Hospital.

After several hours, Bessie was diagnosed as being in severe shock, borderline catatonic. Two more officers showed up at the hospital, and I told them my story while waiting for word on Bessie. Finally, sometime after three P.M., the doctor came out to say Bessie had been given some medication to make her rest, she seemed comfortable, there were no bullet wounds or any other kinds of wounds, externally or internally, and he'd call me tomorrow to let me know how it looked. He said the best thing

13

I could do was go home. He didn't even comment on my bloodstained clothes. I guess to an emergency-room doctor, they didn't warrant mentioning.

Detective Stewart borrowed a car from one of the officers and dropped me off at my place around four o'clock that afternoon. The strange cars that had dotted the neighborhood, in my driveway, Terry's driveway, and on the street, when I'd left hours earlier, were now gone. The news vans, the police cars and vans, the ambulances.

The front door of my house was locked and I didn't have my key, since my purse, for all I knew, was still in the station wagon where I'd left it that morning. I rang the doorbell. In a few seconds, it opened. Willis stood there staring at me.

I've always liked looking at Willis. He's big and blond, with a ruddy complexion and unbelievably dark brown eyes. He's six-foot-two, which fits my five-foot-eleven-inch frame well, and he's a big man, big enough not to be able to buy clothes just anywhere. Which is a pain in the ass. But I don't think I've ever been happier to see him than at that moment. I fell into his arms and burst into tears, and he held me like he didn't even mind that I was still covered in blood and bits of human flesh.

He pulled me into the house and we stood in the foyer, his hands on my face, lifting it up to him so he could look into my eyes. "Baby . . ."

I buried my head on his shoulder, holding on to him like he was my lifeline. My big, burly, brown-eyed lifeline.

While we were standing in the foyer, holding on to each other, the phone rang. Willis kissed my hair, then went to answer it.

"Hello?" He stood in the living room, one hand on his hip, his shoulders slumped. I leaned against the stair banister and watched him.

"Yes, Detective Stewart?" he said after a minute's

14

pause. He sat down in the chair next to the phone and buried his head in his hands. His voice was soft, but I could hear every word, as if my own senses had heightened.

"No, Roy's father left him and his mother when he was like . . . two, I guess. I have no idea where he is or if he's even alive. . . . No, I don't know his name. . . . His mother died last year. . . . No, he was an only child. . . . There was an aunt . . ." He looked at me. "Honey, do you remember the name of Roy's aunt?" He covered the mouthpiece with his hand. "It's the cops. They're trying to locate next of kin."

I got up and walked to my desk. "Roy's aunt's name is Myrtle. I remember that. But she's in a rest home in Dallas." I found my book and looked under *L* for Lester. There we had the names of family to call in case anything happened, just like Terry had the names of my family and Willis'. I read off the name of Roy's aunt and the home where she lived. "And here's Terry's mother." The tears began again. I choked them back, afraid that once they started, they might never stop. "God, Willis, she's right in the middle of chemo . . ." I walked over to him with the book, and he read Mrs. Karnes' name and address in Lubbock out to the police.

"Yeah, she has a sister. . . ." Willis started.

I shook my head. "Remember? Lynda got killed in that car wreck last year."

To the police, he said, "No. I was wrong. No sister. Just her mom. That's all the family either of them had to our knowledge. . . . Okay, thanks."

Willis hung up and came and sat next to me on the stairs. "They want you to come by when you can and sign a statement."

I nodded my head, afraid to speak for fear the tears, like movie Indians, would sneak up and ambush me at any minute.

15

Willis took my hand. "Let's go in the living room, honey, get comfortable."

I shook my head. "Where are the kids?"

"Over at my mother's. They'll stay there the night, maybe tomorrow. Graham's excited about no school."

"Do they know?"

Willis shook his head. "I just told them there were some problems at the Lesters'. That's all."

"Did you find my purse?"

"Yeah," he answered, "I put it on the kitchen counter."

I shrugged my shoulders absently, then said, "I need to go take a shower."

He nodded and I headed upstairs. I found a plastic trash bag under the sink in our bathroom and, taking off my clothes, put them in the bag and sealed it. There was nothing recycleable about those clothes. Turning the water on as hot as I could stand it, I stood under the spray and tried to wash away the evil. I shampooed my hair three times and scrubbed my body all over with a loofah. Still, I didn't feel totally clean. Once out of the shower, I brushed my teeth, used extra cream on my face, and wrapped myself up in my old terry robe. When I stepped out of the bathroom, Willis was sitting on the bed, waiting for me.

"You wanna talk?"

I shook my head, walking to my side of the bed and began rubbing hand lotion into my hands, my back to him.

"You hungry? I could fix you some soup . . ."

"No."

I heard him get up from the bed and go into the bathroom. A minute later I heard his shower running. I took off the old robe, put on a gown and crawled into bed, my back to Willis' side. It was barely 7:30 but I felt as if I hadn't slept in days. Weeks.

16

A few minutes later I felt the shift of the bed as he sat down, then felt his still damp arms going around my shoulders. "How's Bessie?" he asked.

"They can't find anything physically wrong. She's in shock though." I felt his hand stroking my still-wet hair.

"Sweetheart . . ."

"I can't talk about it anymore, Willis, I just can't."

I felt his tightly curled chest hairs through my thin gown as he pressed his body to mine. A while later, he snored gently in my ear. I lay there for hours, unable to move, unable to sleep, just listening to my husband's sounds, the sounds of the house around us, wondering if my children were safe in Codderville with their grandmother. Wondering if we were safe. Wondering if anyone was safe. Ever.

I finally got to sleep sometime after three A.M. When I awoke, it was after ten and I could hear noises, and my mind registered the smell of bacon coming from the kitchen downstairs. I went down in my gown. Willis was leaning against the bar that separated the kitchen from the breakfast room, his back to me, bacon frying in a skillet on the stove against the back wall. He had the Codderville *News-Messenger* in his hands, obviously concentrating hard on what he read. When he heard me walk in, he whirled around, shoving the paper behind his back.

"Let me see it," I said.

"E.J., have some breakfast. I bet you didn't eat anything yesterday. You must be starving. I've got bacon frying and biscuits in the oven. You want your eggs fried or scrambled?" He started puttering about the kitchen, doing his Hannah Hoffrau routine I so enjoy. Not.

I grabbed the paper from where he'd tried to hide it. The headline read, BLACK CAT RIDGE FAMILY VICTIMS OF MURDER-SUICIDE. The story read,

Codderville Police yesterday discovered the bodies of four members of the Lester family of Black Cat Ridge. In an apparent homicide-suicide, the father of the family, Roy Lester, manager of the Codder County Utility, allegedly took a shotgun to his wife, Terry Lester, and two of their three children, Monique, age 16, senior at Codderville High, and Aldon, age 10, fifth grader at Black Cat Elementary, then turned it on himself. The youngest child, Elizabeth, age 4, is in undisclosed condition at Codderville Memorial Hospital.

At this time, the police can find no reason for the apparent murders and suicide.

"You bet your ass they can find no reason!" I said, flinging the paper at the trash. "Roy didn't do that!"

I looked at Willis, his head bent, one massive hand covering his face. "Honey, the police said he was sitting there with the shotgun in his lap, his face—"

I walked up to my husband and gently pulled his hand away. "I know what they saw, Willis, because I saw it first. But that has nothing to do with anything. Roy didn't do it. You know it and I know it."

Willis shook his head, tears streaming down his face. "Ah, shit, baby . . ."

I put my arms around him and held him. And we cried. Both of us. Long and hard. It was the first time I'd ever seen Willis cry, and it stirred something primal in me. Some primal mothering urge I rarely felt even with my children.

Later we sat at the kitchen table with coffee cups before us. "Why would Roy do it?" I asked.

Willis shook his head. "I don't know. He wouldn't . . . not unless he went nuts."

"Why would he suddenly, out of the blue, go nuts?"

Again, he shook his head. I placed my hand over his. "Let's assume for a minute that he didn't do it." Willis

18

looked up at me. "Let's assume," I went on, "that that funny, lovable man we've known for four years did *not* kill his wife and two of his kids."

"If we assume that," Willis the engineer said, "then we must also assume that someone else did."

"Yes."

"And if someone else did, then that someone else manufactured things to make it look as if Roy had done it."

"Yes."

Again, the shake of the head. "But why? Why the fuck would anybody . . . *anybody* . . . do this!"

"It's easier for me to believe somebody else did it than to believe Roy did. So there's a Charles Manson clone out there. I don't know. I just know Roy didn't do it."

This time Willis put his hand on mine. "Honey, statistically speaking, more murders are committed by family members than strangers."

"Not in this case."

Willis stood up abruptly, knocking over his chair. "E.J., we don't know what's in other people's souls, in their hearts! We don't know what went on in their bedroom! What deep dark secrets they had!"

I stood up and glared at my husband. "Well I do! I know they lost a baby between Aldon and Bessie and Roy cried for days! Did you know that? I know that Roy had an affair the first year they were married and Terry kicked him in the balls so hard he had to go to the emergency room! Did you know that? I know that Monique went on the Pill last year! Did you know that? I know that Roy's mother died in an alcoholic ward in Dallas. Did you know that?"

Willis shook his head. "No, I didn't know that. Any of it. Except the ball kicking—Roy told me about that."

"Well, I also know something else. If Roy Lester was capable of doing what was done at that house yesterday, then so are you. So is everybody. And I don't believe that. I could not go on living in this world if I thought for an instant that everyone—me, you, Roy—was capable of what I saw!"

"You don't think *I'm* capable of killing somebody?"

I sat back down. "Yes, I do. I think you would be capable and able to shoot, stab, bludgeon or beat to death anyone hurting me or the kids or even a stranger, but I *do not* think you are capable of picking up a shotgun and chasing your children down the stairs and shooting them in the back!"

The tears were running freely down my face. Sobbing, I got up and left the room, heading up the stairs, feeling the muzzle of an imaginary gun at my back.

Around noon, we got in the station wagon and went into Codderville to pick up the kids. Black Cat Ridge is on a hill overlooking the Colorado River, which separates the new subdivision of Black Cat Ridge from the town of Codderville. We took the back road, a two-lane blacktop from the hill down to the town. After living in Houston most of my life, living on a real-live hill is a novelty. But I wasn't thinking about the hill, or the view, or the bluebonnets poking their heads out in the April sun, or any of the beauty of the part of the world I now lived in. I was thinking about my kids. And what I had to tell them. And how I was going to do that. It was a silent ride. I knew Willis was thinking the same things I was thinking. I figured if he came up with a plan, maybe he'd let me in on it.

My mother-in-law lives in the house Willis' father was born in, an old, frame two-story that's been modernized to the point of having little personality left. Originally it sat on five hundred prime acres, but the land around it has been sold bit by bit over the years until, now, it sits across the street from the back of a K-Mart and two doors down from a mechanic's garage. Graham and Megan love going to Grandma's, though, because she has three dogs and she lets the kids eat all the junk they want.

I remember as a little girl going to my grandmother's house and eating Sunday dinner, which consisted of roast beef, fried chicken, three to four vegetables, two kinds of potatoes and four desserts. Her biscuits, breads and cakes were made from scratch, and the vegetables, if not season fresh, were canned from her garden of the year before. My children's grandmothers, both of them, serve Twinkies and store-bought donuts and cannot comprehend food that can't be prepared in a microwave. But the kids love it.

Graham and Megan were in the back yard, running the dachshund, the cocker spaniel, and the miniature poodle ragged. They heard us pull up and all five, kids and dogs, came charging through the gate to greet us. I held on to my babies a little longer than necessary, felt them beginning to squirm, then let them go.

"So, how's it going?" I asked.

"Grandma bought us pizza for dinner last night!" Megan proclaimed.

"Yeah, and we had sugar cereal for breakfast," Graham added, giving me a look. I didn't allow sugar cereals in our home, and that has been a bone of contention between Graham and me since he was old enough to watch his first Saturday-morning cartoon.

I sighed and stood up, only to catch my mother-in-law glaring down at me from the porch. "Those kids act like you never feed 'em," she said. Coming from normal people, those words are usually spoken in a bantering tone of voice, a "kids will be kids, what are we gonna do with them?" kind of voice. From my mother-in-law, it was a flat-out accusation.

"Good morning, Mrs. Pugh," I said. I call her Mrs. Pugh. Early in my marriage to Willis I'd tried calling her by her given name, Vera, but she'd informed me that she had been married to her husband for twenty-five years (at that time) and in all those years she never called *her* mother-in-law, Willis' grandma, anything but Mrs. Pugh. My mother-in-law has been Mrs. Pugh to me ever since. Occasionally I slip in a Ms., but if she's noticed, she hasn't let on.

"Hey, Mama," Willis said, climbing out of his side of the car and picking both kids up in his arms. "These little monsters giving you fits?"

Mrs. Pugh smiled. "Less than you and Rusty gave me and that's the God's truth."

Willis dragged the kids up the steps to the front porch and kissed his mother on the cheek. She patted his arm and led us into the house. As usual, I took up the rear.

"Everything taken care of?" she asked. She was a firm believer in talking in oblique code in front of children.

Willis nodded. I, as usual, remained silent.

"Good," she said. "Let's have lunch." My mother-in-law is also a firm believer in food healing all wounds. Which I also believe in. I just don't feel *her* food has any rejuvenating powers.

Her luncheon feast was laid out on the kitchen table: nitrate-laden, rat-dropping-infested, store-bought bologna, preservative-enriched white bread, cholesterol-riddled mayonnaise, sodium-saturated potato chips, generic pickles, and a small plate of sliced tomatoes and lettuce, for the sandwiches, I suppose.

I nibbled on the vegetables while my gluttonous family contaminated their bodies. Mrs. Pugh didn't speak directly to me and I didn't speak to anyone. It was the usual warm family gathering.

We got back to the house around three. I had a job to do and didn't know how to do it. I had to tell my children what had happened next door.

Willis and I sat them down in the living room, on the couch together, risking the pinches, kicks and bites that

22

happen whenever they are within two feet of each other.

"We have some very sad news," I started.

Willis nodded. "You know that yesterday something happened over at the Lesters, right?"

Both little heads nodded.

"Well . . ." I said. "Uh, something bad happened . . ."

"I knew it!" Megan piped up. "I knew Bessie was doing something bad. She was all dirty and I bet her mama's gonna beat her butt! She can't play no more, right?"

"Anymore." I took Megan's tiny hands in mind. "Honey, Bessie's not in trouble. She was hurt. She's in the hospital."

The lower lip began to tremble. "She gonna be okay?"

*Hospital* is a bad word in our house. The hospital is where Grandpa went and was never seen again. The hospital is where her beloved Uncle Rusty went after his car wreck. He, too, was never seen again.

I stroked her hair. "Yes, darlin', she's gonna be fine. But her mommy and daddy aren't. They've gone to heaven. And they had to take Aldon and Monique with them."

Graham stood up. "Where's Aldon?" he demanded.

I let go of Megan and tried to grasp Graham's hands, but he pulled away from me, darting out into the middle of the living room.

"Where's Aldon?" he yelled.

Willis stood up and went to Graham, grabbing him and holding him close. Kneeling in front of him, he said, "Son, I'm sorry. I'm so sorry. But Aldon's dead. He's gone. Do you understand?"

Graham squirmed in his father's arms, finally freeing himself and backing away to glare at Willis. "Shut up, you shit!" he yelled at his father.

Megan, still sitting in front of me on the couch, began

to cry. "Mommy?" she said, looking at me. "Mommy, what's a matter?"

I took her in my arms and held her close. How could we tell them this? But how could we not? We couldn't close our eyes and pretend it would all go away. Pretend that Graham wouldn't miss his hero, ten-year-old Aldon, or Monique, his first love. how do you tell a seven-year-old and a four-year-old that children, their friends, are dead? How the hell do you do that? And make it all okay?

Graham pulled away from his father and ran towards the kitchen. Willis started after him, but I said, "Leave him alone. Just let him be."

Willis looked over at us, at little Megan curled up in my lap, the thumb she'd given up a year and a half before firmly wedged inside her mouth.

"This is not going to destroy this family, too," he said, then walked stiffly away towards the kitchen, after Graham.

But the swinging door between the kitchen and the dining room burst open and Graham stood there, his face white, the morning Codderville *News-Messenger* in his hand. Willis stopped and the two stared at each other. "Why, Daddy?" he asked. "Why did Uncle Roy do that?"

With Megan still in my arms, I carried her into the dining room. We all waited for Willis' answer.

"Uncle Roy didn't do it, honey," my husband said. "The police are wrong."

# 3

My kids gave up afternoon naps when each was younger than two. That day, they both took them. Megan cried herself to sleep, after being promised she'd be taken to see Bessie just as soon as the doctor said it was okay. Graham went to his room on his own and shut the door. I have no idea what he did once he was inside.

I left around four-thirty to drive into Codderville to the police station to sign the statement or statements I'd given the day before.

Codderville, Texas, is one of the many small towns that sprang up in the early part of the century to handle all the money spilling out of Spindletop, the single richest oil-field the U.S. has ever seen. Codderville was built along the banks of the Colorado River and became the county seat of Codder County. It was home to many who made a shitpot load of dough off Spindletop. Before they lost it all, they built grand homes in the town. Some still stood. The Codderville Heritage Society was housed in one which had the little Texas seal of a historical monument on its outside wall, a guarantee no one could ever tear it down.

During the 1980s, when the oil bust hit, Codderville went into a slump it may never get out of. Some of the wells in the county are beginning to pump again, but the oilfield supply house, Muster's Derrick Constructions, the Codderville Oil and Gas Cooperative, and many more small oilfield-related businesses are gone forever.

The Codderville County Courthouse was built during the boomtown days of the early part of the century and is made of pink granite surpassed in opulent Texas-style splendor only by the capitol building in Austin. Inside its pink granite walls are the mayor's office, the county commissioner's court, the municipal court, the county court, the county clerk's office, the offices of many lesser bureaucrats, and the police station. An entrance in the side of the building goes directly into the cop shop.

Codderville is not a large town, nor is it a particularly violent one. I didn't know much about the police department and, until the day before, had never had a reason to speak to one of the officers. I've never even gotten a ticket in the three years we've been in the county. I parked the wagon in the little lot next to the police entrance and walked inside. Like so many buildings in the South, this one had been hermetically sealed when central air conditioning was put in. I went from the pleasant seventy-eight degrees of spring weather to an icy sixty-something inside.

The ceilings of the room were at least eighteen feet high. The light fixtures were on long rods coming out of the ceiling and stopping at about normal ceiling height. The counter was made of real wood, oak, chipped and scratched and graffiti-marred, with initials and obscenities poorly repaired. The top half of the walls, above the oak wainscoting, was painted a flat puke green that all but destroyed the effect of the rich wood tones.

People were sitting on wooden benches against the walls, looking forlorn and unloved, just like people sitting on wooden benches in every police station the world over, I suppose. I walked up to the counter to the khaki-clad man standing there filling out forms. He didn't look up.

"Excuse me," I said.

He took his time finishing his form, then slowly lifted his head. "Yesum?"

"I'm here to see Detective Stewart," I said.

"Name?"

"E. J. Pugh."

"Have a seat."

I had a seat, looking as forlorn and unloved as everybody else on the bench. My mind kept going back to the day before, as it had been doing when it wasn't being kept busy with something else. Part of me kept wanting to call Terry and tell her what was going on.

A good fifteen minutes later Detective Stewart came out to get me. Today I looked at him, as I hadn't really registered anything about him the day before. He was two inches shorter than I, and that seemed to piss him off. He was probably pushing the outside of the envelope as far as weight regulations went, if they even still had regulations for such things. His hair was brown frosted with gray and was worn in that super-styled helmet look so many middle-aged men with thinning hair are fond of. As a detective, he was allowed to wear his own clothes. He would have looked better in a uniform. He had on the pants of a green leisure suit (held up with a western tooled belt with the name "Doyle" burned into the leather), gray cowboy boots, and a white shirt of some slinky polyester.

I stood as he walked towards me. He glared up the two inches into my eyes. "Hey, Miz Pugh," he said.

I nodded. "Detective Stewart."

He turned, and I followed him to the end of the counter, through a door, down a corridor and into a bull-pen of desks. His was the one on the right nearest the door. He sat and indicated I take the visitor's chair next to him. He rummaged through the papers on the top of his desk, found what he was looking for, and handed it to me.

"You wanna read this and sign it," he said.

I read. It said everything I'd said the day before, except it left out the mention of my first trip into the house. I said as much to Stewart.

"Shit," he said, then pulled the paper out of my hands and shouted, "Luna!" Back to me, he said, "I don't got the time to hang around here. I'm supposed to be some place. I'm gonna turn you over to another homicide detective. She'll make the corrections and have 'em typed up so you can sign 'em."

"And I'm supposed to wait here while all this is going on?" I asked.

He stood up. "Yep," he said, and as he walked off I came to one giant conclusion. I didn't like Detective Doyle Stewart.

Stewart came back in a minute with a woman he seemed to like about as much as he liked me. She was a Chicana with short, permed dark hair and thick, dark-rimmed glasses, and she stood about six-foot in her one-inch heels. I happily decided she had about ten pounds on me, making her somewhere near 180. I'm very competitive when it comes to my weight. When I find a woman heavier than me, I gloat.

"Luna," Stewart said, "this is Miz Pugh. There's some corrections gotta be made on her statement. I gotta go." And he did.

Detective Luna sat and held out her hand. "Elena Luna," she said.

"E. J. Pugh." We shook.

She grinned. "What's the 'E.J.' stand for, or is that something you don't talk about?"

I shrugged. "Eloise Janine. My husband's just never been able to bring himself to say the name out loud. So it's been 'E.J.' for fifteen years now."

She laughed. "Husbands. They're a real kick in the ovaries, huh?" I laughed while she picked up the statement and read it over. "Shit," she said under her breath. "I didn't realize that thing yesterday was you. I'm real sorry."

I winced. People kept jerking me back to reality. "Thanks," I said. I told her what had been left off the statement.

She shook her head. "BFD. Like this is gonna take an extra ten minutes. Jeez. Some people buck for promotion in the strangest ways."

She added the portion that had been left out in longhand then walked over to the one typist present in the room. She came back and stood over me. "Like some coffee?"

I said, "Sure," and stood up. Detective Elena Luna looked at me, almost eye-to-eye. Then she stepped out of one of her shoes so that we were level.

"No wonder Doyle baby didn't wanna spend any time with you."

"Big women tend to intimidate small men. And I'm not talking about his height."

She grinned. "We're gonna get along fine. Come on back to the lounge and I'll pour you a cup of coffee."

The lounge was down the hall, around the corner, and up a half flight of stairs. Two uniformed officers sat at a back table with their feet up. Luna poured us two cups of coffee and I took a tentative sip, then a bigger one.

"This is good," I said, surprise evident in my voice.

Detective Luna laughed. "I know, I know. Police station coffee is supposed to be terrible. That's what it says on every TV show and movie you've ever seen, right?"

"Right."

"Yeah, well, on TV the cops also have car chases that last fifteen minutes and endanger every citizen on the streets, they carry non-issue weapons, and only wimps follow the rules."

I nodded. "How long have you been with the department?" I asked.

"Ten years. Uniform patrol for nine and a half. Been with homicide about six months."

"How do you like it?"

Elena Luna shrugged. "It's a living."

"What made you decide—"

"To become a cop? Everybody I meet asks that question."

"I'm sorry . . ."

"No, that's okay. I just wish people would ask my male counterparts why *they* decided."

"I see what you mean."

She took a sip of the coffee. "I was an MP in the army. But that was back in the days when they didn't let women carry loaded weapons."

"What?"

"Naw, it's true. I'd be on guard duty—usually with some guy—and I had me an M16, it just wasn't loaded."

"That's the stupidest thing I've ever heard!"

She grinned. "That's the U.S. Army." She shrugged. "It's better now, though. They actually issue women ammo. Anyway, when I got out I realized I liked the work, I'd just have preferred if it was real. So I went to the police academy."

I suddenly realized I'd been storing away the things Luna and I talked about. Filing them in the little drawer in my head marked, "Things to repeat to Terry." How long would it take for all of my brain to know she was gone?

"You got kids?" Elena Luna asked.

I nodded. "Two."

"Me, too. Two boys."

"Boy and a girl."

She grinned. "They both got that red hair?"

Why is it when you're a redhead, people comment on it? I've never noticed people commenting on the color of other people's hair—*"Where'd you get that brown hair?" "Everybody in your family a dishwater blonde?"* I guess people figure if you're obnoxious enough to have red hair, then that gives them the freedom to comment. I've often thought of changing the color, but I just can't think of anything else the freckles would go with.

"Actually," I answered, "my daughter's hair is a combination of her father's and mine. Kind of a strawberry blond. My son's hair is a little darker than mine, but almost as bright."

"Yeah, well, it's real pretty." She looked at her watch. "Tammy should be through with your statement. Ready to go back?"

I nodded, not all that certain I wanted to read the damned thing again. Once back in the bullpen, Luna retrieved the statement, which I read and then signed.

Checking her watch again, she said, "Well, I'm off duty. I'll walk you to the car."

We took a shortcut through a door marked POLICE PERSONNEL ONLY and ended up right in the parking lot where my car was. She walked with me to the wagon.

"I'm really sorry about what you had to go through, Mrs. Pugh."

I took a deep breath. "Roy Lester didn't do it," I said.

"Ma'am?"

31

"I read the paper this morning. The police say it looks like a homicide-suicide. It's not. Roy didn't do it."

Elena Luna looked down at the ground for a moment, then back up at me. "I know how hard this kinda thing is to accept, Mrs. Pugh—"

"You didn't know him. I did."

"Yes, ma'am. Well . . ." She opened the car door for me.

I just looked at her. "You're not believing a word of this, are you?"

"Mrs. Pugh, it's not my case. I really don't know any more about it than the average citizen."

"Whose case is it? Stewart's?"

She sighed. "Yes, ma'am."

I got in the car and rolled down the window while she shut the door. "Detective Luna," I said as I started the engine, "there is someone walking around Codderville very much alive who killed four people yesterday. I just hope you're aware of that. And I hope you're aware of the fact that there's a little girl lying semicomatose in the hospital who could have been a witness to the whole thing. What about her?"

As I drove out of the parking lot, I saw Elena Luna's face in my rearview mirror. She was shaking her head in pity. And I was getting pissed.

# 4

When I got home, I fixed the kids an early dinner and sent them to bed, Megan with her thumb in her mouth, Graham with a scowl on his face.

Willis was in the living room watching TV. I cleaned up the kitchen and turned off the lights. As I walked through the kitchen and into the breakfast room, the window facing Terry's house beckoned me. I walked over, turned the louvers of the miniblinds open and stared at the house next door.

It had been so good. Us and our neighbors. We had a lot of friends in Houston, but we'd never had friends in our married life like Terry and Roy. It happens in life that two people click when they first meet. But four? It happened with us. Terry was my best friend. Roy the big brother I never had. Roy was Willis' best friend. Terry his cross to bear. The one who pushed his opinion buttons. The one who got him started and laughed until he quit. How many times had I seen him fake-strangle her, swat her butt, all those things he would never do with a woman "friend." Except Terry.

I felt the presence behind me. Smelled him, the husband smell that's in his pillow I lay my head on when he's out of town. Willis put his hands on my shoulders and leaned against me, both of us looking out at the house next door.

"It's just like Rusty . . ."

I turned and looked at his eyes. Willis rarely talked about Rusty, his little brother. His mother handled Rusty's death by talking about him incessantly, like he'd just gone down the street for a pack of cigarettes. Willis handled it by pretending Rusty had never existed. I didn't know what to say. Whatever words I chose could be the ones to shove Willis back in his shell. But not talking could do the same.

"We'll get through it, just like we did with Rusty."

He pulled away from me and sat heavily down on the couch. "You have any idea how pissed off I am about Rusty?"

"I think I do."

He shook his head. "No, you got no idea! I mean, Jesus, Eej, he was only twenty-one years old."

I sat down beside him.

"He had his whole frigging life ahead of him."

I took his hand in mine and began rubbing a finger along the fine white-blond hairs on the back of his hand.

He pulled his hand away and, standing up, began pacing the living room. "It's been two years, babe. I'm not even beginning to deal with Rusty yet. How in the hell do I deal with this now? Huh? You have any idea about Roy and me? How I felt about that guy? It was like, having Roy—my friend—it was like almost getting Rusty back. And Daddy, too." He stopped and looked at me. The dark brown eyes were darkened further by the dampness of the tears he was holding back. He never cried for Rusty.

Maybe that's what he was doing now. "Eej, Roy didn't do it."

I shook my head. "No, honey, he didn't."

"He didn't kill Terry and his kids."

I stood up and walked over to him, wiping a strand of blond hair off his brow. "Nope. He didn't."

He sighed. "I can't stand much more."

I put my arms around him and held him. I couldn't stand much more either.

I left the house shortly after that, heading for the hospital to check on Bessie. When I'd said what I did to Detective Luna, it was the first time I'd put that fear into words. Either out loud or to myself. Bessie could be in danger. And nobody believed me.

When I got to the hospital I found Bessie the same as the last time I'd seen her. Lying in the bed, her dark hair contrasting sharply with the white sheets, staring up at the ceiling, her hands at her sides. She was clean—that was the only difference. I inquired at the nurses' station about a private duty nurse. That, at least, would be something. Some kind of shield between Bessie and the beast. I left feeling sick to my stomach, wondering what would happen to that beautiful, gentle child.

On Wednesday, Willis went back to work and I kept the kids home one more day. Which may have been a mistake. Graham stayed in his room most of the day, coming out only to eat. Megan dogged my every step and would go into a crying jag if I tried to go to the bathroom alone.

At noon on Wednesday, Reverend Rush called. Willis and I had let Terry and Roy talk us into going to church with them the first year we moved to Black Cat Ridge. Mrs. Pugh wanted us to attend the First Baptist in Codderville. As I was baptized Episcopalian, I had some extreme reservations about going Southern Baptist. But since both of us felt the children needed some religious training, we

35

compromised and went with our friends to the Black Cat Ridge Methodist.

We were delighted when we went to our first service and found the preacher a very liberal woman named Beth Asbury. We went every Sunday and became very involved and never did find out if there were any rules to being Methodist. You didn't have to kneel like you did at the Episcopal church where I was raised, and you could dance, as opposed to the church where Willis was raised. But then Beth moved on, to a bigger church in Houston, and we've been stuck for the last three years with Berry Rush, a right-wing pro-life activist.

The only thing worse than Berry Rush is Rosemary Rush, his wife. Separately, they are both pompous, arrogant, self-righteous, and holier-than-thou. Together, they're royal pains in the ass. We stayed only because the youth director, Kenny Dayles, is great with the kids. And we figure maybe we can outlive the Rushes.

"E.J.?" he said when I picked up the phone. "This is Reverend Rush."

One of the things I found obnoxious about the man was that, even after three years, no one, to my knowledge, was allowed to address him as Berry, with the possible exception of Rosemary, and we weren't terribly sure about her.

"Oh, hello," I said, finding the nearest chair and sitting down. Along with everything else, Reverend Rush was long-winded.

"I was so terribly sorry to hear about what happened at the Lesters."

"Thank you."

"Do you have the names of the next of kin so I may call and offer my condolences and any services they might possibly need?"

I excused myself and got my address book, reading off

the names of next of kin, the same names we'd given the police.

"I understand you found them, E.J."

"Yes."

"How are you doing?"

"I'm . . . okay, Reverend Rush. Thanks for asking."

"If there's anything Rosemary or I can do . . ."

The thought made me shudder. "No, really, I'm all right. But I do appreciate your concern. While you're talking with Mrs. Karnes, Terry's mom, if you would, ask her to contact me . . . if there's anything I can do."

"Certainly," he said, and hung up.

If I knew anything for certain, I knew he'd never mention my name to Mrs. Karnes. I stayed where I was by the phone, address book on one knee, Megan on the other, and dialed long distance to Lubbock, hoping to beat Berry Rush to the punch. The phone was picked up on the second ring.

"Hello?" a female voice said.

"Mrs. Karnes?" I asked.

"I'm afraid Mrs. Karnes can't come to the phone," the lady said. "She's not taking any calls right now."

"Oh, of course. I'm sorry . . . ah, this is E. J. Pugh. I was Terry's next door neighbor . . ."

"Oh, my goodness! You're the poor thing that found . . . Oh, my goodness."

"Yes, ma'am. Look, if you'd just tell—"

There was a commotion on the line. I could hear the woman say, "Now, Irene, you shouldn't be up . . . E.J., Mrs. Karnes wants to speak to you."

I heard the phone pass from one to the other and I gulped in air, wondering what the hell I thought I was doing.

"E.J.? Is that you?"

"Yes, Mrs. Karnes, it's me."

I heard her sob. "I don't believe any of this," she said.

"I know, I know." I hadn't realized how hard this was going to be. My own tears were welling up and spilling over. This woman had been through so much. So goddamn much.

"How's Bessie? Are you taking care of Bessie?"

"She's still in the hospital, ma'am, but I saw her yesterday. It's too soon for the doctors to know much." Know what, I hope she didn't ask. She couldn't take the possibilities. The horrible possibilities that went through my mind a million times a day.

I heard her take a breath. "Do you have a copy of their will?" she asked.

"No, ma'am. I don't know that they made one."

She sighed. "Well, they did. Last Christmas when they were up here. I made them. When I found out the cancer had come back, I told them I couldn't be responsible for those children. I figured, you see, that I'd be dead long before . . ."

"Yes, ma'am . . ."

Again, the intake of breath. "Terry didn't talk to you about this?"

I shook my head, saying, "No, ma'am."

"Well, you and your husband are executors of the will, dear. Lynda was, but then . . ." She sobbed. "A woman shouldn't outlive both her children, E.J.! It's not right!"

I was gasping for my own air. Terry hadn't said a word. Not a word. But then, when was there time? Why would that be on her mind? Her sister dead, her mom dying. Why would she even think to mention it?

"I hate to break it to you like this, E.J.," Mrs. Karnes was saying. "You're listed as guardian of the children in case . . . oh, Lord."

I scooted Megan off my knee and stood up, only to have her grab me around the leg with both arms. I dragged myself and her over to the kitchen counter and poured myself a cup of coffee, black.

"Mrs. Karnes . . ."

"I can't be responsible, don't you see?"

"Ma'am . . ."

"E.J., I'm dying. The chemo . . . isn't working. They're talking about putting me back in the hospital."

"Mrs. Karnes, I'm so sorry . . ."

"Thank you, but that's not the point. The point is Bessie. Now I have a lawyer up here and I'll have him send you the will . . . maybe fax it, is that what they call it?"

"Yes, ma'am."

"Anyway, you need to get to a lawyer yourself. Somebody's going to have to pay for Bessie's hospital bills . . . and the . . . funerals . . ."

"Mrs. Karnes, we'll take care of it," I heard myself saying, not believing I was actually saying it. "Please don't worry about it."

"Oh, I'll worry about it, E.J., I'll worry myself sick, but there's not a blasted thing I can do about it! About any of it!" I heard another deep intake of breath, as if she were fighting for each one. "E.J. Roy . . . Roy was like a son to me . . ."

"He didn't do this, Mrs. Karnes."

I heard her sob again, then the phone went dead in my ear.

Dragging Megan behind me, I went into the living room and fell on the couch. I couldn't believe Terry hadn't said a word. But when I thought about it, really thought about it, who else was there? Lynda, Terry's sister, had been killed the year before in a car wreck. She was single, a lawyer in Lubbock, and had been the one who was to take the children in case of Terry's and Roy's deaths. Terry had been so broken up over Lynda's death that the thought about the children's future had never entered my mind. Somewhere there might be some cousins, but no one close, I knew that. If there had been,

39

surely Mrs. Karnes would have talked Terry and Roy into using family.

I sighed. What the hell was I going to do if Bessie ended up in the hospital for life? What was I going to do if she didn't? I didn't look forward to breaking this news to Willis, the man who asked if it was okay if he took off for a couple of years when I informed him of the imminent arrival of Graham. He'd been kidding. Of course.

Willis now had responsibilities with a capital *R*. And I knew it scared him. Every day in every way, it scared him. How could I now tell him he was responsible for another life, one we didn't bring into this world, one we just inherited? Not to mention the responsibility of the Lesters' house and their belongings, the funerals, and everything else that went with being executors of an estate. People die from things like this. They get high blood pressure and high cholesterol, have heart attacks, strokes, aneurysms, and die.

I put Megan down for a nap and tried to work. When I was pregnant with Megan, we needed a little extra money. That's when I started writing romance novels. They were something I could do at home, in between children's naps, laundry, and meals. And, I discovered, it's something I'm good at. I'm now pulling in about twenty grand a year to supplement our income. Since Willis started his own business, that "supplement" has bought groceries on bad months. I have an office (a converted closet, actually) under the stairs between the breakfast room and the kitchen. In it, I have a small computer table, my Mac, one filing cabinet, and a list of titillating adjectives taped to the wall.

I loaded the Mac with my current project, reading back to the beginning of the chapter. Ah, yes, Chapter 14, wherein Lady Leslie is accosted by the sexy hunk she believes to be the footman but who is actually Lord Maynard in disguise. I skimmed over the wet-panty portion, finding where I'd left off, with the two idiots still not consummating anything. "She tore herself from his arms, her velvet bodice ripping in his hands, knowing this could never be. No matter how much her body lusted for the firmness of his arms, the curve of his thighs, her station in life would not, could not, allow it."

I typed, "She ran through the woods, feeling the heat of his gaze on her back, his eyes undressing her as surely and as deftly as his hands had attempted to do only moments before." Then I erased it.

As if my fingers had minds of their own, I got a clean screen and started doodling. "An ordinary suburban family. Parents and 2 kids. He works for the city government. A nothing bureaucratic job. She's a housewife. They're all found dead. A shotgun"—and I stared at what I'd done. I erased it, turned off the Mac, and went and sat in the living room.

Was I playing detective or gathering information for a "true life" crime novel? I didn't know. Was I a concerned and loving neighbor or a sick and evil voyeur? I didn't know. I needed to discuss this with Terry, that was for damn sure. I put my head in my hands and cried.

I felt little arms around my neck, a little hand patting my back. "It's okay, Mommy," Megan said. "Heaven's a wunnerful place. They got angels and Jesus and everything." Again the pat. "It's okay."

I pulled her into my lap and hugged her hard. "Thank you, honey," I said. "You are absolutely right." I kissed her dirty cheek, then spit-washed it with my finger. "You want to help me fix dinner?"

While Megan and I puttered around the kitchen, Graham came in and crawled up on one of the high stools, sitting there, silently watching us. At one point, walking by him, I ruffled his hair with my hand. He jerked away and made a face. Things were getting back to near normal.

41

Willis and I lay in bed that night staring at the ceiling. The kids were finally asleep. Dinner eaten, dishes done, television watched. Not-so-glad tidings told. ''I don't fuckin' believe it,'' Willis finally said.

''Honey . . .''

''I don't goddamn fuckin' believe it.''

''Who else is there?''

Willis sat up in bed. ''I don't know! And I don't care! Just so long as it's not us!''

''They loved us like family. We loved them that way, too.''

Willis got out of bed and began pacing, his sorts riding up the crack of his ass in that funny way they have of doing. Finally, he stopped and looked at me. ''I keep thinking, 'I'm gonna get him for this.' Like, it's some practical joke and next week I'm gonna get him back by greasing his sander or something.''

''Willis . . .''

''What if Bessie's never better? What if she stays like she is now? What are we going to do?''

''We'll deal with it. She's our child now, honey. There's got to be insurance for this, though. My God, he worked for the damn county! He had the kids insured! I'll call them tomorrow.''

Willis nodded.

''And I'll call a realtor about selling the house.''

He shook his head and said, ''We need to wait on that. Until we have the will and it gets through probate.''

''I know we can't put it on the market, but we can get an estimate.''

He nodded. ''Yeah, I guess we can do that.''

''And after I call his insurance at work, I'll go by the hospital—I need to go see Bessie anyway—and I'll get things straightened out with them,'' I said.

We both jumped when a noise from downstairs interrupted. We looked at each other. "The refrigerator," I said.

Willis nodded and laid his head back down. "What we need is a burglar alarm system."

"How much would that cost?"

He lifted up on his elbow and looked at me. "I can't believe you can think about money when our family's lives are at stake."

I lay down and looked up at the ceiling. "You're right. But a burglar alarm system seems so . . . constrictive."

"You'd prefer bars on the windows?"

"No. Of course not." I sighed. "An alarm sounds fine."

He nodded and laid back down. He mumbled, "I'm gonna get Roy for this." In ten minutes he was snoring softly and I suddenly realized I couldn't sleep at all. Not with thoughts of bells ringing in my ears and all the responsibility I'd just taken off Willis' back and heaped onto my own.

# 5

"Roy Lester . . . *L-E-S-T-E-R*. Lester. . . . Yes, I'll hold."
So far I'd talked to the receptionist at the County Utility, the secretary to the Board of Directors of the County Utility, the secretary to the head of the employee relations department of the County Utility, and now I was on the phone with the employee relations insurance clerk. Finally, she returned to the line. "Ma'am, I'm sorry, but I cain't give you no information on Mr. Lester 'less he gives me his permission in writing."

"Look," I said, my anorexic patience wearing exceedingly thin, "as I've explained to just about anybody who will listen at your company, Mr. Lester is dead. Do you read the papers?"

"Ma'am?"

"The newspaper. Or watch TV?"

"Ma'am?"

Why didn't anybody who worked with him know Roy Lester had been shot to death and was accused of taking his family with him? "Mr. Lester is deceased," I said slowly, "so, therefore, he will not be able to write to you to give you permission to give me the information I need. Are you with me so far?"

"Look, lady, you don't got no call gettin' snotty with me."

I sighed. "I'm sorry," I said, "I don't mean to be snotty. But it's taken me quite a while to get through to you, and I just need to explain what's happening."

"Look, I don't gotta put up with guff from nobody."

"I understand that. Is there a supervisor I might speak with?"

"One moment please."

And I was on hold. Again. After a good five minutes, I heard a voice say, "This is Mrs. Harp. May I help you?"

"Mrs. Harp. Hello. My name is E. J. Pugh and I'm the executrix of the estate of Roy and Terry Lester. Mr. Lester is the late manager of your utility."

"I'm aware of that."

"Good. As you may have read in the papers, his youngest child, Elizabeth, is in serious condition in the hospital. As executrix of the estate, I need to assure the hospital that the bills will be paid. I assume Mr. Lester had his insurance through the utility?"

"We'll need confirmation from Mr. Lester's attorney, ma'am, that you *are* the executrix of the estate before we can give out any information."

"I understand you won't be able to pay the bills until you get such information, Mrs. Harp, but all I want to do now is to be able to assure the hospital that there is insurance so they won't toss Elizabeth out in the street. The child is very ill, Mrs. Harp, and she's only four years old."

"Well, maybe Mr. Lester should have thought about that before he took the shotgun to his family, Mrs. Pugh.

I'm sorry, there's nothing I can tell you at this time. Good-bye."

I sat there with a dial tone buzzing in my ear, wishing I'd gone down there in person so I could slap her face. I was so mad that, as I put down the receiver, my hands were shaking. And I knew instantly that I was going to have to become very thick-skinned to get through this. For Bessie's sake, if not my own. I was sitting there, my hand still on the phone, Megan still on my lap, when the phone rang, jarring me so that I almost dropped my child.

"Mom!" she said, in that tone of voice she used for incredibly stupid behavior on my part. The first sign of my baby getting back to normal. I kissed the top of her head and picked up the phone.

"Hello?"

"E.J.?"

"Yes?"

"Reverend Rush here."

Oh, goodie. I repressed my baser urge to reply, "Berry, baby!" and instead simply said, "Hello, how are you?"

"Very well, thank you. How are you?"

"Fine." I sighed. I would ask no more questions. With Berry Rush, you could go on like this for days.

"I spoke with Mrs. Karnes."

There was a silence. Finally, I said, "Yes?"

"She said she had just spoken with you."

I felt as guilty as necessary, then said, "Yes. She was quite upset."

"Of course. I understand you and Willis are the executors."

"Yes."

"Then you and I must get together to make funeral arrangements."

I sighed. "Yes, I suppose so."

"I think we should consider a private funeral with closed caskets, under the circumstances."

47

"Closed caskets, certainly. But why a private funeral?"

"Under the circumstances, E.J., I'm afraid we'll be inundated with curiosity seekers."

"That is certainly a possibility," I said, consciously speaking as pompously as the good reverend. "But Roy and Terry had a lot of friends in this town. I wouldn't want anyone to think they were being slighted. Everyone has a right to say good-bye."

There was a silence. Finally he said, "I really think a private funeral would be best."

The first year Berry and Rosemary Rush had come to Black Cat Ridge, Willis, Roy, Terry, and I, as members of the executive committee for the purchase of playground equipment for the Sunday school play yard, had found a wonderful company that supplied safe playground equipment made of recycled plastics. The way churches work, the congregation is the boss, the pastor an employee. We had spent months finding the right equipment and were quite happy with our presentation to the church board and the new Reverend Rush. In his oh-so-kind-aren't-I-the-most-reasonable-man-in-the-world bullshit voice, Berry Rush managed to blow us clear out of the water. To this day, the kids still have the old steel-girder playground equipment, and once a year someone gets hurt. A month later, the parsonage had a large family room added to it. But I'd be goddamned if he was going to do it to me this time.

"Well, if you really think so, Reverend Rush. I suppose we can get Reverend Bailey at the Codderville First Methodist to officiate and have the service there."

"Now, E.J. . . ."

"I know it would be best at Black Cat Ridge Methodist, but I understand your feelings."

There was a silence. I smiled into it.

Finally, the Reverend Mr. Rush said, "Of course I'll officiate, E.J. If you want an open service, then as executrix, that is your prerogative. I would just like to go on record as opposing the idea.''

''So noted,'' I said.

''Why don't we get together—'' I heard the rustling of his busy schedule ''—tomorrow. Threeish?''

Again I smiled. ''My children get home from school threeish, Reverend Rush. Could we make it in the morning?''

Again the rustle. ''Friday, ten A.M.''

''Fine.''

''Good-bye, E.J.''

I was still grinning when I hung up the phone. We take our little victories where we can.

Willis got home from work early, dragging in like he'd just lost his best friend, a giant box in his arms, his briefcase perched on top.

I suppressed my urge to run to him with slipper, pipe, and paper in hand. No reason to set a precedent.

''What's that?'' I asked, indicating the box.

''The burglar alarm system,'' he said, dropping it on the floor next to the front window.

''I thought we were going to have it installed,'' I suggested.

Throwing his briefcase on the couch, followed by his body, he said, ''Ha! You know how much that'd cost? I can install the fuckin' thing myself and save us a bundle.''

I'd heard that one before. From the automatic garage door opener to the ''little assembly required'' toys we bought the kids at Christmas. After several hours of exclamations ranging from, ''I can't believe somebody would build something this poorly! If I designed something for an oilfield like this, I'd be out of business in a New York minute,'' to ''If I'd known I had to speak Japanese to assemble a fuckin' Big Wheel, I'da gone to Berlitz!'' I'd get mad, he'd get madder, we'd fight, the

49

kids would cry, and we'd end up hiring someone to come in and take it off our hands. I thought about mentioning his words to me of the night before—"I can't believe you'd think about money when our family's lives are at stake"—then thought maybe I'd just hire a German shepherd guard dog to patrol the halls at night. It would save wear and tear on the marriage.

I sat down on the couch next to him and he slipped his arms around my waist, squeezing tightly.

"God, what a bitch of a day," he said into my hair.

Megan was on my lap before the words were out of his mouth.

"Honey, why don't you go play?" I suggested.

"No."

"You want to go to your room and play with your Barbies?"

"No."

"You want to go outside and play on the swingset?"

"No."

"Graham!" Willis yelled toward the stairs. "Come get your sister!"

We expected the usual ten-minute debate about how he wasn't paid enough to baby-sit Megan, how he had his own business to tend to, how she was nothing but a brat who tried to break his things, on and on ad nauseam, but instead, Graham walked down the stairs, came up to us and held out his hand for Megan. She looked at me first, trying to see if I thought it was possibly a trap, then dutifully left with her brother.

After they'd made their way upstairs, with Willis and me both staring dumbfounded after them, he said, "What's wrong with Graham?"

"He's not himself."

"That's obvious."

"Okay," I said, relegating my children to the nether regions of my mind, "tell me about your day."

"Well, I got a call from Roy and Terry's lawyer in Lubbock."

I sighed with relief. "Great. I haven't been able to get anywhere about the insurance. Not without his written verification that we're the executors."

"It's in the mail."

I nodded. "Was it bad?"

Willis shrugged. "He didn't know them. Barely knows Mrs. Karnes. Just wrote up her will. Then theirs when they were in town. Just going through the motions."

"Have you noticed something curious?"

He put his arm around me and pulled my head down to his shoulder. I've never liked doing that. I'm almost as tall as he is, taller sitting down, and the posture hurts my neck like crazy. But, naturally, I've never mentioned it.

"What's that?" he asked.

"I haven't heard word one from Paul and Marilou. Or anybody else for that matter." Paul and Marilou Tanner were friends from the church, people who'd known the Lesters almost as well, and definitely as long, as we had.

"Somehow, I think we're alone out here. Nobody else wants to get involved. Maybe they think it's catching," Willis said.

I lifted my head and looked up at him, smiling sweetly. "Well, at least we have Berry Rush."

Willis started laughing and I joined him. And we laughed until the tears came. Again.

Early the next morning I awoke with a start, wondering if Willis had heard me scream. I looked over at him, lying on his side, facing away from me, snoring lightly, oblivious to my horror. My nightgown was stuck to my body with sweat, and I could smell myself. Not a pleasant experience. I went into the bathroom and turned on the light, wincing from the glare, and ran cold water in the sink, splashing it in my face and rubbing a cold washcloth over my chest and pits and neck. I shuddered, remembering the dream.

Megan and Bessie were playing with their Barbies on the floor in the living room. Monique was supervising, laughing at the little girls. Graham and Aldon were running up and down the stairs, Teenage Mutant Ninja Turtling all over the place. Aldon holding his cringing Leonardo, poised for flight; Graham charging with a growling Shredder.

Terry and I sat at the bar in the kitchen, sipping iced tea and laughing. The sliding glass door to the patio opened and Willis came in, looking over his shoulder at Roy behind him. When Roy came into view, he had no face. Just the quivering red hole where one used to be. And I screamed.

But obviously not loud enough to wake up the asshole I slept with. I opened the bathroom door, the light still on, letting the brightness flood our bed. He snored on. I opened it wider, banging it against the wall. Nothing. Finally, realizing games were not going to work, I went to the bed, crawled over to him and hit him on the shoulder. "Willis, wake up!"

"What— . . . ?"

"Wake up!"

He opened an eye and tried to focus on me. "Wha . . . ?"

"I had a nightmare!"

He turned, valiantly trying to grasp the situation. "You okay, honey?"

"No, I'm not okay!"

He sat up and rubbed his face. "You had a nightmare?"

"Yes."

He reached out a hand and touched my hair. "I'm sorry. You want to talk about it?"

"No."

"Oh. Then why did you wake me up?"

52

Well, he had me there. I stared at my hands. Finally, I shrugged. "I guess I just didn't want to be alone."

"You're not."

"I am when you're asleep."

He pulled me to him, his hands beginning their trek up and down my night gown. I pulled back. "I don't want to make love," I said.

His hand worked its way under my gown, rubbing my bare back. "Might take your mind off the nightmare."

I got up and went into the bathroom, shutting the door behind me. I turned off the light and sat down on the bathmat. In a few minutes I heard his gentle snoring again. I sat there and fumed, planning how I'd tell Terry about it in the morning over coffee. Then I cried.

# 6

Thursday morning dawned as one of those few perfect days we get in Texas that make living through the rest of the year tolerable. Perfectly clear blue sky, temperatures in the high sixties in the morning, high of the day to be no more than mid-seventies, a light breeze from the southeast.

I woke up with an isolated feeling of dread. Something was wrong. I just didn't know what. In a few minutes, reality came, and with it, memory. I got out of bed and started my morning with a vengeance, a firm believer in mindless activity pushing away dread. Something I learned from my mother. My father in the hospital having his first bypass surgery. Mother in the kitchen, on her hands and knees, scrubbing tiles.

Here it was Thursday, and I hadn't even looked at the Lester house since Monday. Much less been inside. I'd been parking my car on the street to avoid the mutual driveway. It was supposed to be an unconscious thing.

But I knew I was doing it. Avoidance is a learned trait and I'm a real quick study.

I got the kids ready for school and drove them there, both somewhat subdued. It was going to be rougher probably on Megan than Graham. Megan and Bessie were in the same class at the Montessori. Graham and Aldon had been far enough apart in age that they rarely socialized at school.

After I dropped them off at their different schools, I went quickly to the post office, where a certified letter from Lubbock awaited me—the official notice that Willis and I were executors of the Lester estate and, therefore, entitled to entry into their personal business. I left the post office and went immediately to the building that housed the Codder County Utility. With the piece of paper in my hand, I didn't even have to speak to anyone special. Just show my piece of paper and they gave me a letter stating that Bessie was covered at 80 percent for hospitalization, that there was a $200,000 life insurance policy on Roy (no suicide clause, since he'd been employed there and had had the insurance for over ten years), and that Roy's retirement account stood at $156,-000. With this information in hand, I left the Codder County Utility and headed for the Codderville Memorial Hospital. Once at the receptionist's desk, I asked to speak to the hospital administrator.

The lady working the receptionist's desk was obviously a volunteer, a gray lady, and gray she was—from the top of her head to the bottom of her sensibly shod feet.

"The hospital administrator?" she asked, her voice incredulous. "You want to see the hospital administrator?"

"Yes, I would," I said. I smiled. She didn't seem to be able to figure out how to return it.

"Well, just a minute." Instead of picking up the phone and calling someone, she got up from the desk and stopped a woman in a business suit walking down the hall towards us. I heard her say, "Mrs. Jaynes, this lady wants to see the hospital administrator!"

Mrs. Jaynes said something back to the gray lady that I didn't catch, but it certainly seemed to impress the gray lady. She came back to the desk, sat down, picked up the phone receiver, and punched in some numbers. Clearing her throat, she said, "There's someone here to see Mr. Marshall." Her face turned red and she said, "I don't know. Just a minute." Punching hold, she looked at me, "Who are you?"

"E. J. Pugh. I'm here on behalf of one of your patients, Elizabeth Lester. In pediatrics."

She punched a button, said, "Oh, dear," and redialed the administrator's extension. "I'm sorry. This is reception again. Her name is E. J. Pugh . . . about a child . . ." She looked at me.

"Elizabeth Lester," I supplied.

"Elizabeth Lester," the gray lady said, heaving a sigh that she'd gotten through yet another battle. She listened, then said, "Thank you," and turned to me. "Go down this hall to where you see the red line on the carpet. Follow the red line until you see the sign that says 'Administration.' Turn right. Follow the green arrow and turn left at the blue arrow. It's the third door on the right. It says, 'Administration.' "

"Do you have a map?" I asked.

The gray lady said, "Oh, dear!" and started rummaging through the papers on the desk.

I reached over the counter and touched her hand. "I'm sorry. I was just kidding. I'll find it. Thank you."

She nodded her head at me in great confusion, and I left, following the red line, the green arrow, and the blue arrow.

Once I found him, Mr. Marshall didn't appear to be all that inaccessible. He sat in his shirtsleeves in an office without a secretary, the door open, crunching numbers on a ten-key. When he felt my presence in the doorway, he looked up and smiled.

He was about twenty. Okay, maybe twenty-five, but I doubt if he shaved more than once a week. "Mrs. Pugh?" he asked, standing and coming around the desk, his hand extended.

I shook his hand and took the chair he indicated. "What can I do for you?" he asked.

I showed him the papers from the attorney and from the personnel department of the utility. "Just to let you know there won't be any problems in paying for Elizabeth's care."

"Well, I'm sure glad you came by with this. You won't believe how many people think this stuff is free." He laughed. I smiled.

"Since the insurance only pays eighty percent, we'll need a personal check for the difference before she checks out. I hope you understand."

My stomach fell. I knew we'd get the money back, eventually, but with Willis owning his own oilfield engineering consultancy firm, we were as close to broke as anybody could be and still have a roof over their heads.

I smiled. "No problem," I said. "How much do you think it's going to be?"

He smiled back. "Let me check." He picked up the phone and dialed an extension. "Hey, Bette, it's Bruce." Checking a computer readout on his desk, he said, "What are the current charges on number 137429-PED?" He waited. I waited. The whole world waited. "Okay, thanks."

He looked at me and smiled. "Looks like they're releasing her as of tomorrow. That's good news, huh?"

I smiled back. "That's wonderful news."

"So," he turned the ten-key on and crunched my own

58

personal numbers. "Off the top of my head, I'd say the twenty percent will come to . . . $1,375.82."

A housenote and one utility bill. I stood up. "Well, I'll go see Elizabeth now and talk to her doctors. You'll have all that ready tomorrow when I check her out, right?"

He stood up. "No problem, Mrs. Pugh. And we really appreciate your concern for the child and for the bill."

He got that in reverse order, I'm sure, but I let it slide. We shook hands again and I left, going back down the blue arrow, to the green, to the red line, back to reception and to the bank of elevators that would take me to the fourth floor and pediatrics.

Bessie was sitting up in bed and a girl in a candy striper uniform was feeding her Jell-O.

"You are such a brave little thing," the girl said. "You're my brave Bessie. Look at how you eat this stuff! Why, you're the best little girl on this whole floor, you know that?"

I smiled and said, "Hi."

The girl looked around and blushed. "Hi," she said.

I came into the room and kissed Bessie on the cheek. "Hey, Bessie, honey, how are you doing?"

She didn't answer. She didn't smile. What she did do was look at me. Right into my eyes. I thought my heart would break wide open. "You're going home tomorrow, honey. Back to my house! Megan's so excited. We'll fix up the extra bed in there just for Bessie. Like when you spend the night. How does that sound?"

She leaned forward, taking the Jell-O from the spoon in the candy striper's hand into her mouth. She squashed it around a minute, then looked at me and nodded.

"Can I have a hug?" I asked. She put her little arms around my neck and squeezed. Real live communication.

As she let go, I kissed her cheek again. "I'm going to go see your doctor, then I'll be back, okay, honey?"

She didn't respond but went back to her Jell-O. The

nurse at the station said the doctor was in the lounge, but she'd call her and for me to have a seat in the waiting room. I did. This was a different doctor than the one I'd seen in the emergency room. Probably the pediatric resident on staff. Her name was Ashma Rajahri and she was one of those women other women would just as soon not be seen in the company of. She was about five feet two inches tall, weighed maybe eighty-five pounds sopping wet, had jet black hair in a braid, the end of which tickled the backs of her knees. And she had a face that would make a grown man weep. When she smiled I decided I'd give up my left tit just to look like her.

"You are the Lester child's guardian?" she asked, her English as perfect as everything else about her.

I handed her the paper from the lawyer. "Ah," she said. "Very good. It is such a tragedy. I am very sorry for your loss."

"Thank you. I just want to say, though, what a great job you've done. Elizabeth looks wonderful!"

Dr. Rajahri smiled. "Do not thank me. Thank the incredible recuperative powers of children. She is a very brave little girl."

"Yes, she is."

"One thing you should be aware of, Mrs. Pugh," the doctor said, leading me to one of the couches, where we both sat. "Elizabeth is not speaking. I don't know how long she will be thus, but as of now, she is not talking. There is nothing wrong with her physically. I had an ENT specialist check her out, and there is nothing wrong. Yet, she does not speak."

"You can't say how long . . ."

Dr. Rajahri shook her beautiful head. "I only wish that we could. I would suggest that at your earliest convenience, you seek psychiatric counseling for the child. She has been through a very traumatic experience and I can only assume this is what has made her speechless."

I nodded my head, wondering how Megan was going to handle this. How any of us was going to handle this.

When I got back to Bessie's room, she was napping. I sat for a minute, just watching her. Was I going to be able to love her as much as I loved my other two? How good a mother was I, anyway? How in the hell did I expect to be able to take on a troubled child, when I could barely deal with my own two? Would Bessie grow up thinking of Megan as my *real* daughter? Would she call me "Mom"? *Could* she call me "Mom"? Could she call anybody anything? I had to hope I'd be as good a mother to Bessie as Terry would have been to my kids. Only Terry would never have gotten my kids. They were going to my older sister, Candy, to be raised with her three. I guess I'd better tell Candy she'd have a sixth now, if anything happened to Willis and me. Maybe that's what I should do. Give the kids to Candy and run off to Japan to become a hooker. I've heard Japanese men love big American women. And redheads. I put my head in my hands and started crying. I seemed to be doing a lot of that lately.

I got myself together and used the bathroom in Bessie's room to wash my face. I'd given up wearing makeup the last few days. I never did do a very good Tammy Faye imitation. I kissed sleeping Bessie good-bye and left the hospital, going to Johnson-Remey Funeral Home. Johnson-Remey was in another of those wonderful old houses built during the boom. A three-story Victorian with turrets and wraparound porches. I'd made calls the day before, figuring out which of the two funeral homes in town would let the bill ride until the estate money came through. Naturally, the more expensive one was the more generous. They'd told me on the phone to come by anytime to pick out caskets.

I parked in the parking lot at the side of the minimansion and walked around to the front door. I guess I expected to be greeted by a tall, thin, middle-aged man with a deep voice (John Carradine in his prime). Instead, I was greeted by a fight. A short, pudgy man in his mid-fifties, wearing suit pants and shirtsleeves, tie loosened, was giving hell to a younger man in bluejeans and a white smock. They weren't exactly in the foyer, but standing in a velvet-draped doorway to the right of the entrance.

"I tole you! You wanna do Hollywood, move to California! I don't want none of that stuff on my people!"

"It's just your basic dusty rose base—"

"That woman looks like a clown! You want her family coming in here seeing her look like a clown?"

The guy in the smock stiffened. "I really resent your tone, Mr. Remey."

"I resent your fairy-assed butt!"

"My wife will be real interested to hear you think I'm a fairy!"

"Well, she should be! I want that lady scrubbed off and redone! Human lookin', you hear?"

I coughed discreetly. Both heads turned in my direction. Mr. Remey motioned the young man in the smock away and straightened his tie. A professional smile started, stopped, and started again on his face. He walked towards me, his hand extended. "I'm Horace Remey. How may I help you?"

I shook his hand. "I'm E. J. Pugh. I believe I spoke to you or your partner on the phone. Concerning the burials for the Lester family."

He nodded his head. "Such a tragedy! Such a terrible waste."

"Yes. . . . Uh . . . I guess I need to look at some caskets. I spoke to someone on the phone about delayed payment . . ."

"Of course. When dealing with estates, we often work out something with our bereaved." He pointed toward a velvet drape in the center of the foyer. "Our viewing room."

62

He ushered me into a large room full of caskets; big ones, little ones, wood ones, metal ones, shiny ones, dull ones. I planned on going medium, all the way. We walked around while he told me the virtues of the top of the line, a mahogany number with white satin tufting on the inside, guaranteed water-resistant for up to one hundred years. I figured that to get the full benefit of the warranty, one would have to dig up one's loved one every ten years or so to check.

This was all new to me. No one in my family had died as of yet, except for one grandfather, who died when I was twelve and I had nothing to do with that funeral. Willis had taken care of the arrangements for both his father and his brother, but I hadn't been involved in anything other than fixing food and trying to be supportive. This time, it was all on my shoulders. I figured, hey, I'm five-foot-eleven, weigh 170 pounds: my shoulders should be big enough.

I selected the caskets. Three adult-sized oak cases with tufted sateen lining. With a fifty-year guarantee. One child-size casket, painted white, with a blue sateen lining. We arrived at a figure that took my breath away, but I signed on the dotted line. I figured I was in this for the long haul.

I spent the evening with my family, not telling anyone about the cost of the day. The hospital bill of over $1,000, the bill that would be coming from the funeral home for more money than I made on three books. I don't know why I was shielding Willis from the financial side of this. Maybe for fear that he'd leave me. I'd never thought about it before. About Willis leaving. But I guess I wasn't all that sure of his strength. It had never really been tested before. Oh, I knew he could bench press three hundred pounds on a good day because I once saw him lift a clothes drier in anger and fling it across the garage. But intestinal fortitude? That I wasn't sure of. Dealing with the death of family members is one thing. Dealing with the details of the deaths of friends—that was something else entirely. That was something one could reject. Would Willis reject it? Would he reject Bessie? I didn't know. And I didn't want to push it to a conclusion. So I kept quiet. Because I'm a chicken.

Early in the evening I took Megan to the hospital to see Bessie. Dr. Rajahri said it would be okay if I snuck her in. There were no contagious children in or around Bessie's room.

On the ride over, I told Megan, "Honey, Bessie's not talking right now. She's sick and she can't talk. Do you understand?"

"Why?"

"Why what, honey?"

She sighed. "Why can't she talk?"

"Because she's sick."

"She got a sore troat?"

How does one explain psychological repression to a four-year-old? Answer: One doesn't.

"Yes, Megan, she has a sore throat."

As we were driving along, I noticed Megan looking out the window, up into the not quite dark sky.

"Honey," I asked, "what are you looking at?"

"Where are they?" she asked.

"Who, honey?"

"Aldon and thems. Are they in the clouds? Do the airplanes run into them up there in heaven? Can we take a airplane to heaven? How come they don't fall down? Can you walk on clouds? Do they have bottoms?"

I looked straight ahead of me, turning into the parking lot of the hospital, letting Megan run on and on and on.

Finally, she said, "Mommy!"

I turned to look at her. "What, honey?"

"How come the airplanes don't hit heaven?"

64

"Because heaven's higher than airplanes go," I answered.

"Then what about spaceships, huh?"

Well, she had me there. "Spaceships go right by heaven and don't even know it's there."

"Why?"

Where was Reverend Rush when I really needed him? "Just because," I answered. She's only four. She accepted it.

We snuck up the back stairs, Megan delighted at the long flights, her mother exhausted as we reached the fourth floor. We made it into Bessie's room without being noticed. The private duty nurse I'd hired sat in a chair beside Bessie's bed reading a *Ladies' Home Journal*. Bessie lay back on her pillows watching *The Cosby Show* on TV.

"Hi, Bessie!" I greeted as we entered the room. The nurse put down her magazine and Bessie looked up. "Look who came to see you!"

Seeing Megan, she didn't smile, but she did lift her hand up in a small wave. Megan ran over to the bed. "You sick?"

Bessie nodded her head.

"You gonna get better?"

Bessie shrugged her shoulders.

"You're gonna come live with me!" Megan announced.

Bessie looked at her.

Megan's pouty look came to her face. "You wanna, don'tcha?"

Bessie shrugged her shoulders.

Megan turned to me, a not-so-nice look on her face. "Mommy!"

"Sit, Megan. And don't talk so much. Bessie's not feeling too well." I took Bessie's hand in mine. "Honey, we love you very much and we're going to be very happy to have you come stay with us."

Bessie's hand lay limply in mine. How much did she know? How much should I tell her and when? And how did I keep Megan from blurting it all out? By leaving quickly, that's how. And talking at some point soon to a shrink.

"Well, honey," I said, "we just came by for a minute to say hi. I'll be back in the morning to get you, okay?"

Bessie shrugged. I kissed her on the cheek, watched as Megan did the same, and then took the brat home and to bed.

Later that night I lay in my own bed trying to sleep. Willis lay next to me, his reading lamp on, a sheaf of papers spread out on his lap. He had a bid to make the next day. An important bid. One that could mean whether or not we ate during the month of June.

I was at that point—somewhere between sleep and wakefulness—that twilight state. I saw the hospital corridor. Dark, light from the nurses' station spilling shadows on the industrial carpet. I saw the private duty nurse going down the hall. On her back. Someone was dragging her by the hair . . .

I sat up in bed, gasping. Willis pushed his reading glasses down on his nose. "What?"

I jumped out of bed.

"E.J. What's the matter?"

"I have to go to the hospital."

"Honey?"

He took the glasses off and laid them on the covers, watching as I tore off my gown and slipped on sweats.

"E.J. Visiting hours are over."

"She's not safe there!"

Willis got out of bed and came over to me. "Honey, she's fine."

"She's a witness! If Roy didn't do it, and I know he didn't, then somebody else did and Bessie is a witness!" I took a deep breath. "They may try to eliminate her."

66

Willis burst out laughing. I swear to God. He laughed so hard he fell back on the bed, holding his sides.

"You asshole!" I said, grabbing my shoes and socks and heading for the door.

"Honey! My God! You realize how silly that sounds?"

"About as silly as what happened next door." With that, I left, hoping reality might sober him up.

There was no gray lady at the reception desk. Instead there was a guard. Complete with gun. My story planned, I ran up to him. "The doctor just called. My child's taken a turn for the worse. I have to get up to pediatrics. Fourth floor."

"Yes, ma'am," he said, leading me to the elevators and punching the fourth-floor botton.

"Thank you," I said as the doors closed. I only felt a little guilty.

Once on pediatrics I looked down the long corridor. It was better lighted than in my dream, but not much. The nurses' station was empty. My feet made the only sound as I walked down the empty corridor. I opened the door to Bessie's room slowly. The room was dark. A hand grabbed my arm and flung me to the floor.

# 7

I felt a heavy weight on my chest. Then the lights were turned on, blinding me momentarily. When I could see again, I saw Bessie standing on tiptoe by the light switch.

A voice said, "Well, Eloise Janine, how nice of you to join us."

I looked up into the face of Detective Luna, who sat astraddle me.

"Would you mind getting your fat ass off?" I asked.

"You don't have to get personal," she said, sliding off and standing up, one arm extended to me. I took her outstretched hand and yanked myself up off the floor.

"If I've ruptured a vertebra, who do I sue, you or the city?" I asked.

Bessie scurried back into bed, sitting up and watching us, her cocker spaniel brown eyes taking in everything.

"Have to be me personally. I'm not on duty."

"Then what the hell are you doing here?"

She shrugged and went over and sat in the chair next

to the bed. She held up the book she was reading, *Natasha's Secret Desire*. "A little birdie told me," she said, grinning big. " 'Fear gripped her in her most holy of places, a warm fire spreading through her loins.' " Detective Luna looked up. Off-tune she sang, "Holy, holy, holy . . ."

I grabbed the book out of her hand. "Not in front of the *c-h-i-l-d*." I sat the book down on the bedside table. "What are you doing here, Luna?"

She shrugged, squirmed, and turned a darker shade. It was my turn to grin. *"I'm* just this crazy lady," I said, "with this crazy theory about . . . you know what. Whatever can a big-city detective be doing here?"

"On the off chance you could be right . . . I thought I'd just . . ." She waved a hand as if swatting away her embarrassment. "Anyway."

"Were you here last night?"

Elena Luna and Bessie exchanged looks. Bessie looked at me and nodded. I grinned again. "Bessie goes home tomorrow. You gonna come stay with us for a while? I can fix up the sofa bed in the living room."

"Go to hell . . . ma'am." She shrugged. "My mom's in town for a couple of weeks. She's staying with the kids. I didn't have anything better to do . . ."

"Luna, admit it. Admit you just *might* believe me!"

Again she shrugged. "There's always the possibility you're not totally wacko."

I bowed. "Thank you."

"You're welcome. Now get out before I call hospital security. You're not supposed to be in here."

I kissed Bessie good night. "Get some sleep, honey," I said and headed for the door.

"She was—before you burst into the room."

I started to retort but decided I'd let her have the last word. I can be unbelievably generous at times.

On the way home, I stopped and bought three candy

bars. All chocolate. I'd given them up over a year before, but stress is the great enabler. I'm a secret chocoholic. I stash chocolate all over the house, only eating them after the kids are in bed. How could I ever get Graham to eat non-sugar cereal again after he's seen me wolfing down a Snickers? I ate the 3 Musketeers on the way home and hid the M&Ms and the Hershey's bar in the back of the freezer for later, then joined Willis, who was reading in bed.

I crawled in the bed and kissed him. When that was over, he lifted one of my lips and looked at my teeth. "You have a piece of chocolate stuck on your incisor." So much for my stealth.

The next morning, before my ten o'clock appointment with Reverend Rush, I needed to do something. I needed to go into the house next door. Bessie would need clothes, toys, and other essentials. After I dropped the kids off at school, and before I dressed for my meeting with the Right Reverand, I took the key off the inside of the door to the Tupperware cabinet in my kitchen and, steeling myself, walked from my back door to Terry's back door.

The large, square kitchen was the same. The butcher block–looking Formica counter tops, the Mexican-tile floor, the almond appliances. Terry's thatched-roof canisters lined the back of one counter in precise stair-step fashion, the matching cookie jar a space over. A spider-web had formed in the corner of the stainless steel sink. Glass canisters of spaghetti and four different kinds of pasta lined another counter in stair-step fashion. A letter and a couple of bills were stuck between the spinach noodles and the rigatoni. A bottle of Tylenol stood on top of the refrigerator, on the front of which were childish drawings not unlike the ones on my own refrigerator, hanging there with the help of magnets shaped like Garfield, a basket of flowers made of dough, a ceramic praying hands, and the like. The stove top was clean, the spice rack above it only slightly greasy.

But the kitchen smelled. I opened the refrigerator and discovered part of the problem. Another part was in the pantry—where Terry kept the kitchen trash can. Bones and rinds were doing their thing against the ozone layer. I gathered the garbage, adding to it the perishable items from the refrigerator, and dragged it into the garage, where Roy kept his larger cans. From there, I dragged all of it out to the curb. I went back to the kitchen, looked under the sink for the Lysol, and began spraying. It helped the smell. It didn't help the fact that I still had to go up the stairs to Bessie's room to get her things.

I knew, standing there in the kitchen, that the blood would still be on the walls and stairs and in the two bedrooms. No one had come in to clean. And I doubted if the cops would have straightened up before they left with the bodies. At this point, I could do one of two things: bite the bullet and go up the stairs, or go to the mall and buy Bessie everything new.

I headed toward the stairs. Breathing through my mouth and keeping my eyes on my feet, I hugged the inner wall—the clean one—of the stairwell and made my way upward. I tried not to think of the feelings crowding in on me, not the least of which was the overpowering feeling of being somewhere I didn't belong. I'd been in Terry's house before when she wasn't there. When the family was on vacation and I came over to water the plants and bring in the mail. Even then I'd felt that strange feeling of isolation, of total aloneness. Now it was almost stifling. That and the smell that assaulted me even though I tried to breathe only through my mouth.

I averted my eyes from everything until I got to Bessie's room, where I ran inside and began grabbing the necessary items. But leave it to a four-year-old not to have matched luggage. There was nothing to pack it all in.

72

Why didn't I get a Hefty bag while I was messing with the garbage? Because I'm stupid, that's why. Okay, at this point there were again options: I could go downstairs and get said Hefty bag, or I could go into Terry and Roy's bedroom and into the master closet where they kept their luggage and get a suitcase.

I went downstairs and got a Hefty bag. The silence, the utter complete silence of the house was getting to me and I began to notice that my own movements were hushed: walking on my tiptoes, lifting things gingerly so as not to make a sound. I grabbed the Hefty bag, rattled it loudly and, on my way back up the stairs, began singing Chuck Berry's "Nadine," one of the few songs I know all the words to. It helped.

Back at my house, I took the clothes and bedding to the laundry room. The stale smell of the house next door permeated the clothes. Or maybe just my nose. Anyway, I wanted them washed. With the bundle under my arm, I headed for the washer. There on top sat a manila folder.

I dropped the clothes and looked at the folder. Friday, after school, while Terry was gone picking up the little kids, Monique had come over, asking me to hide the folder for her. I opened it. Inside was an imitation-leather-bound book with "Journal" stenciled in genuine faux gold on the front. I leaned against the wall, the tears beginning to spill yet again.

I'd loved Terry as much as, if not more than, my own sisters. But she had her flaws. One of them was not giving Monique the privacy any teenager is due. Of course, I'm not yet the mother of a teenager, so that's easy for me to say. But I never agreed with Terry's rummaging through Monique's drawers and closets, looking for her secrets. That's why, the year before, I'd agreed to let Monique receive mail here at my house from a boy I knew her parents didn't approve of. He dropped out of school the year before and joined the Marines. They corresponded regularly for three months, a letter every two days arriving at our house, and then one of them, Monique probably, found a new love, and the mail-drop became a thing of the past.

But obviously, Terry had been going through Monique's drawers again and Monique hadn't felt it safe to leave her diary where her mother could get her hands on it.

I stroked the imitation leather and the faux gold lettering. Little Monique. So bright and pretty and, oh, God, so funny. Like the time when she was thirteen and reading her first trashy novel. She'd sneak over to my house and we'd talk about it, since I wrote trashy novels.

She looked at me with those big cocker spaniel brown eyes of her mother's and said, "Ginny is just putting on a facade."

"A what?" I'd asked. She'd pronounced the word *"fuc-aide."*

"A facade."

I pronounced the word correctly and she blushed. "Oh," she said finally, "I guess I was thinking about a telethon for hookers."

I laughed until I thought I'd cry. And I couldn't share it with Terry. That was the bad thing. Only Monique and I had known about the trashy novels.

I put the journal back into the manila folder. I'd save it for Bessie. It would be a way for her to know her big sister. I stuck the manila folder on the top of the shelves in the laundry room, picked up Bessie's bundle and loaded the washer.

Later, I made up the extra bed in Megan's room with Bessie's own Peanuts sheets and comforter and pillow, stuck her stuffed Big Bird and Bert and Ernie on the bed, and cleaned out two drawers of Megan's four-drawer chest, putting Bessie's undies and things inside. I hung the few hang-ups I'd brought in Megan's closet. I mean,

Megan and Bessie's closet. Then I put Bessie's new coloring book and her favorite storybooks in the bookcase.

Fifteen minutes later, dressed in my good jeans and an oversized cotton sweater, I drove to the church and my meeting with Berry Rush.

His office, in a new annex next to the church, built with the funds originally earmarked for the dilapidated Sunday-school wing, was plush. A teakwood desk, a six-foot silver and teakwood cross on the wall between rows of built-in bookshelves, an antique settee and a winged rocker. The asshole. He met me at the door with outstretched arms. Two of them, grabbing me by the shoulders and squeezing.

"E.J. It's so good to see you! I'm so sorry it had to be under these circumstances! Come! Sit! Coffee? Tea? A cold drink? Possibly milk?"

I did everything expected of me and declined the offer of refreshment. I pulled the paper from the Lubbock lawyer out of my purse and showed it to him. "This proves power of attorney."

"As if I would doubt it?" He chuckled.

"Now about the services."

"Since you insist on an open affair, I suppose we should have it in the sanctuary. The chapel would be too small for the hordes of curiosity seekers liable to attend."

I smiled stiffly. "I doubt if we'll have that many. Now, about the service . . ."

"I've selected some hymns I feel appropriate for the occasion." He then read off three of the drier selections in the Methodist hymnal, a hymnal that specializes in particularly dry hymns.

I shook my head. "I don't feel—"

"I've spoken to Choir Leader Johnson. He feels under the circumstances a soloist would be out of the question. A few flowers, possibly. Sedately scattered."

"Reverend Rush." My voice was loud, so as to be heard above his.

"Why, yes, E.J.?" His look of hurt surprise would have withered a lesser person.

I shoved a piece of paper in his hand. On it were written three song titles. "These were Terry's favorite hymns. These are the ones I want sung at the funeral."

He laughed nervously. "But these hymns are inappropriate for a funeral, E.J."

"I really don't give a shit, Reverend Rush. These were Terry's favorite hymns. These hymns will be sung in her honor. And I'm sure as a friend of Roy's, Tom Johnson would be happy to do the solo honor himself on 'Amazing Grace.' As for flowers, there will be no flowers. People will be instructed to give any money they want to donate in the Lester family's memory to the Codderville Children's Foundation, a favorite charity of Terry's. You know she worked there as a volunteer. Also, they will be buried at the Memorial Hill Cemetery. Plots were bought there years ago. I'll have to see about getting two extra for the kids. But Terry and Roy already have plots there." I stood up. "Now, if you'll kindly draw up a bill for the use of the church and your services, Reverend Rush, and mail it to me, I'll be happy to add it to the pile of other bills awaiting probate. Good day."

I left the room to an amazing quiet. Not a sound. Not a peep. It took every ounce of willpower I had not to turn back for a look.

I went from the church to the hospital where I wrote a rubbery check for $1,375.82, the 20 percent insurance wouldn't pay, and retrieved Bessie. I dressed her in red jeans and a blue top with red and yellow balloons, helped her with her socks and tying her Junior Keds, and picked her up and hugged her.

"You ready to go to my house, honey?" I asked.

Bessie didn't respond. Did she want to ask questions?

Did she want to ask, "Where's Mommy? Why can't I go to *my* house? What the hell's going on?" I smiled and set her down, taking her hand and leading her out of the hospital room and down the corridor to the elevator.

"Bessie! Honey, you leavin' us?" called a nurse.

Bessie turned her head and smiled, lifting her hand in a gesture of farewell. The candy striper from the day before came out of a room down the hall and ran up to us. "You leaving, Bessie-wessie?"

Bessie nodded. The girl hugged her. "I'm sure gonna miss you!"

Bessie hugged her back and we made it to the elevator. I called thanks to everyone as we stepped inside and headed back to Bessie's new home.

When I pulled up to the curb in front of our house, Bessie didn't even glance at her house, sitting quietly next door.

I got Bessie tucked into bed with Bert under one arm and Ernie under the other, with Big Bird sitting at the foot of the bed facing them all, keeping track of what was going on.

"You wanna take a nap?" I asked, stroking her hair away from her forehead.

She nodded, turned to her side and closed her eyes. I left the room. I'd noticed the daily Codderville *News-Messenger* on the driveway as we drove up. I went outside and got it. I hadn't looked at the news since Monday. I wondered what page my friends warranted by Friday.

Page one. But at the bottom. I sat in the kitchen sipping a warmed-up cup of coffee and checking out the front page. The death of the beloved Mrs. Olson, the counselor at the high school Monique had attended, in a strange car accident had bumped the Lester family from the top of the page. That and an article about possible misappropriations at the Codder County Utility. A small article in the right-hand corner was all the news fit to print about the

Lester family. "Police sources say they are wrapping up their case on the Lester family murders, which will be listed as murder-suicide."

I threw the paper in the recycle bin. Fuck a bunch of 'em, I thought. Nobody was going to do anything. Nobody! Four people murdered and everybody in Codderville was just going to look the other way. I picked up the phone and called the police station, asking for Detective Luna.

"Detective Luna," she said, picking up the phone.

"I read the paper this morning."

"I'm glad you're able to read, Mrs. Pugh. It's astounding the number of adults in this community that can't. You should be congratulated. Possibly the Adult Literacy Program at the high school could use your—"

"Can it, Luna. I'm not in the mood for what you consider humor."

"Is there something I can do for you, Mrs. Pugh?" she asked, her voice sickly sweet.

"You can get off your duff, you and the rest of the jerks at that place, and find out who killed the Lester family!"

"Mrs. Pugh. After an exhaustive investigation—"

"Of less than four days," I interjected.

"—we have discovered nothing to prove anyone else was involved in the murders of the Lester family. There was no break-in—"

"They rarely locked their doors."

"—no indication of a disturbance of any kind. No neighbors heard anything—"

"No one asked me!"

"Did you hear anything, Mrs. Pugh?"

I sighed. "Well, no, but that's not the point."

"And—and this is the kicker, Mrs. Pugh—and Roy Lester was found with the murder weapon in his possession in a position of suicidal indication. Therefore, the verdict has been handed down that Terry Lester, Monique

Lester, and Aldon Lester were murdered by Roy Lester, who then shot and killed himself."

There was a long silence. Finally, Detective Luna said, "E.J., I'm sorry. I know this is not what you want to hear."

"Look, Detective. I know that's what it looks like because that is precisely what it is *supposed* to look like! But I'll tell you one goddamn thing for sure, and you can take this to the bank: Roy Lester did not kill his wife and kids."

"You come up with any proof of that, ma'am, and we'll be happy to reopen the case."

"You know," I said, "I'm sitting here thinking, what in the hell do you do when you can't get the police to investigate a murder? Well, I've just figured out what it is I'm supposed to do! I just remembered. I think the Codderville *News-Messenger* might be interested in a little muckraking of the police department. They might be interested in the truth!" And with that, I hung up.

I went upstairs to find Bessie sitting up in bed having Bert and Ernie engage in a nonverbal argument. They were doing a lot of jumping up and down and Bessie was doing a lot of glowering for them, but little else was happening.

"Hi," I said. She put the dolls down and looked at me.

"I need to go on an errand. You wanna come along?"

She nodded her head and crawled out of bed, slipping her shoes on her feet and holding them up for me to tie. She learned to tie her shoes a couple of months ago, but a little regression, I figured, after what she'd been through, was to be expected. I figured as long as she didn't have to be re–potty trained, I was ahead of the game.

I drove straight into downtown Codderville to the *News-Messenger* office, a small building in the shadow of the courthouse, a hop, skip and jump from Detective Luna's den of inadequacy.

A friend of my mother-in-law's worked the reception desk and I dropped Bessie off with her. With all the woman's cooing and goings on she might not even notice Bessie didn't speak. Then I headed back to the office of Armstead Pucker, editor and general manager of the Codderville *News-Messenger*. Armstead already thought I was a bit looney-tunes after trying to get his support in starting up a local chapter of the National Organization for Women. He went so far as to put the ad we paid for in the paper (to which we—Terry and I—got no response), but as for printing any of the articles I brought him, he declined.

Armstead Pucker was my age, mid-to-late thirties, and about as beige as a person could get. He was medium height, medium to pudgy in build, had light brown hair receding rapidly, a fair complexion, and absolutely no distinguishing marks. One could only hope he never went missing. He had a round, cherubic face that should have had dimples but didn't. When he saw me standing in the doorway to his office he smiled. With his mouth. His eyes held no expression whatsoever. Armstead Pucker was one of those people who, when you looked at him, you wondered if anyone was home and, if there was, would it be worth the bother of ringing the bell?

"Armstead, hi. Remember me, E. J. Pugh?"

"Yes."

"May I come in a moment?"

"Yes."

I walked in and sat down in the chair across from his desk. I almost asked for a cup of coffee but was afraid he'd say yes.

"I'm here to talk to you about the Lester family."

"Yes?"

"I'm not sure if you're aware of this, but Roy Lester didn't kill his family."

He nodded his head. I doubted if it was in agreement—it probably was a way to encourage me to continue. What Armstead Pucker didn't realize was that I needed no encouragement.

"Roy Lester was a devoted family man. He loved his wife and children to distraction. But not in any irrational way. What I'm saying is, Roy didn't do this. There is no way."

"Mrs. Pugh. Neighbors usually say things like this."

"Yeah, right. 'Good old Charlie Manson, he was such a nice quiet guy.' That's not what I'm talking about, Armstead. I'm saying that there is someone here in our community who has murdered four people, two of them children, and the Codderville Police Department is doing absolutely nothing about it!"

"Do you have any proof . . .?

I threw my hands up in distraction. "No I don't! But, goddamn it, I'm gonna get some! I'll hire a private detective!"

I stormed out of his office, rescued Bessie from the ministrations of Yolanda Pace, and went home.

# 8

I woke up Saturday morning around seven-thirty. The house slept around me. I checked on Megan and Bessie and found them both sleeping soundly. Megan had recently started sleeping in to around eight. A blessing.

I went downstairs and made coffee, then went out and got the paper, on the driveway between the two houses. The one thing I wanted to do more than anything in the world was go knock on Terry's door and for the two of us to have a quiet cup of coffee while the families slept. And to tell her about it. To tell her how scared I was, how worried. How damned much I needed her.

I picked up the paper and looked at the house, sitting there in the early-morning sun, just like every other house on the block. But it seemed now to have an air about it. Something tangible. Somehow, I knew, a stranger coming onto the block could look at that house and know it was deserted. And know, too, that something had happened there. Something bad.

I turned away and went into my kitchen and poured my first cup of coffee. I sat down at the kitchen table and pulled the rubber band off the Codderville *News-Messenger,* opening it to the front page. A banner headline read:

NEIGHBOR SAYS LESTER FAMILY MURDERED
VOWS TO HIRE INVESTIGATOR TO GET AT TRUTH

I involuntarily spit my mouthful of coffee across the room. Grabbing the paper in my hands, I read:

Mrs. E. J. Pugh, neighbor and executrix of the Lester estate, claims that Roy Lester did not kill his family and then himself, as police sources have indicated. Mrs. Pugh cites possible cover-up by the Codderville Police Department. "At the very least," Mrs. Pugh said, "they've dropped the ball royally on this one."
Vowing to hire a private investigator, Pugh claims there is evidence to prove the Lester family was killed by outsiders. Mrs. Pugh lives at 1411 Sagebrush Trail in Black Cat Ridge and is the wife of Willis Pugh of Pugh Oilfield Engineering Consultants here in Codderville.

My hands were shaking and my coffee was getting cold. The fact that Armstead Pucker had the gall to identify me as "the wife of Willis Pugh of Pugh Oilfield Engineering Consultants" got my feminist dander up. The fact that he listed my address scared me shitless. What did he think he was doing? Who in the hell did he think he was?

The phone rang. I grabbed it before it could ring again. "Hello?"

"Incredibly smart, Mrs. Pugh."

"Luna? Is that you?" I realized I was whispering and wasn't sure why.

"You've really stepped in it this time. If you think

84

you'll get any cooperation from the department now after what you said in the paper . . ."

"I didn't say any of that! Armstead made it up! I mean, I don't *think* I said any of that. Jesus, Elena, I was just ranting, for Christ's sake!"

"Well, you'll be the laughing stock of the county and that's for damn sure!"

Okay, laughing stock was going entirely too far. "Why? Because I loved and trusted my friends and can't believe them capable of unspeakable acts? That makes me a laughing stock?"

"What's going on?"

I looked up to see Willis standing in the doorway, his hair sticking up in spikes atop his head, his newly acquired gut hanging over the top of his pajama bottoms, his feet bare, rubbing his eyes for all the world like another four-year-old.

Into the phone, I said, "I gotta go. Bye," and hung up. I grabbed at the paper spread out before me to hide it, but Willis grabbed it first.

All of a sudden, he no longer looked like a benign four-year-old. He definitely looked like a malevolent thirty-eight-year-old. He sat down heavily in one of the kitchen chairs.

"What the fuck?"

"Honey . . ." I started.

He glared at me. " 'Mrs. Pugh vowed to hire a private investigator.' " He looked up from his reading. "You *what?*"

I shrugged. "I was just sorta talking, you know, and, well, Armstead must have taken some of what I said seriously, though of course he had no right to."

"Do you have any idea what this is going to do for my chances of getting that bid? It's gonna skunk my chances, that's what it's gonna do. You know Harry Martin, owner of Wildcatters, Inc.?" I nodded my head, although I felt it was probably a rhetorical question. "You know Harry Martin's real big on law enforcement? You know Harry Martin's an honorary deputy and donates thousands every year to the Widows and Orphans Fund of the police department?"

He threw the paper down and walked out of the room.

Willis stopped speaking to me. We didn't discuss it. We just didn't talk. I wanted to discuss the fact that we were now sitting ducks if our theory that Roy didn't do it had any validity. I wanted to point out that we might, just might, be in danger. But Willis preferred sitting on his fat ass in front of the TV watching golf (which he doesn't even play) rather than speak to me.

By three o'clock I'd· had enough. I herded the kids together and told them we were off. From the foyer I called in to my very own couch potato, "I'm taking the kids to the movies."

He grunted at me, then sat up, smiled brightly at the kids and said, "Have a great time!" Thus making sure everyone and their brother knew I was being excluded because I'd been a bad girl. The asshole.

I said, "If you get tired of watching the golf match, you could always *attempt* to install that damned burglar alarm." There. I'd cast aspersions at his masculinity. We were even.

Disney had recently re-released *101 Dalmatians*. Bless 'em. Graham wanted to go to the R-rated Arnold movie, but my clout and the fact I was the one holding the money won him over.

Bessie was holding on tightly to the Ernie doll, which hadn't been out of her hands since the moment she found the three dolls in the room she now shared with Megan. I bought Cokes, popcorn, and Junior Mints and we set about blowing the afternoon.

Disney cartoons have a way of making me forget my troubles. I was laughing and booing Cruella De Vil right along with the kids. We got out of the theater a little after five and started home. It had been bright and sunny and close to eighty degrees when we'd gone in the theater. But Texas being Texas, when we got out it was raining, as my late father-in-law was fond of saying, like a cow pissing on a flat rock. As I'd left the driver's side window open a couple of inches, my seat and the floor were drenched. Grabbing Willis' trouble towel out of the compartment under the floor of the cargo area, I dried it off as best I could and we set off for home.

Willis and I met in 1973 at the University of Texas in Austin. Our junior year. We fell madly in love while staring at each other across the room at the Co-op Bar and Grill on the Drag. We continued to stare at each for more than a week as we regularly began to bump into each other. After this lengthy courtship, we moved in together at the close of our second date. But that was the way things were done back in those days.

One night, towards the end of our first month together, we went to see a revival of *Bullitt* at the theater on the Drag, while under the influence of acid, which we had been told by many was the proper hallucinogen under which to view this particular film. Afterwards, we took Willis' 1968 VW to the parking lot of the football stadium and practiced 180-degree turns at high speed. Willis never did get it right. But I was great. It was one of the big thrills of my life. I had that VW spinning like a dreidel every time I tried it. Willis, of course, decided it was a dumb thing to be doing and decided he'd rather go back to the apartment to eat and get laid. Which is what he most enjoyed doing while on acid anyway. Or any other time, for that matter.

There is a reason for this journey into the wicked past of the Pugh parents. The kids and I left the parking lot of the mini-mall where the theater was and headed out Highway 12 towards Black Cat Ridge. The rain was coming down in sheets, my windshield wipers were on phase 2, and the kids were arguing as usual. Well, at least Graham and Megan were. From what I could see in my quick glances in the rearview mirror, Bessie was sitting quietly between the two, walking Ernie across her knees.

We were nearing the bridge crossing the Colorado River that separated Codderville from Black Cat Ridge when a black van pulled up beside me on the four-lane road. At first I paid no attention. When he swerved, hitting my left front fender, my attention was gained.

I stepped on the brakes, slowing the wagon down, only to have the van slow down and swerve into me again, pushing me towards the bridge abutment. A second's glance into the window of the van showed me only my own reflection: all the windows appeared to be tinted in black.

Flashing to my *Bullitt* training, I hit the brakes as hard as I could, cut the wheel, and pulled a true 180, heading down the highway in the wrong direction. With two of the three kids screaming in my ears, I bumped over the divider in the highway, getting to the correct side, the van more slowly following my example.

I have a fairly new American wagon. It weighs a couple of tons. It does not go fast. I've gotten it to seventy miles an hour while on open highway on family vacations. I pushed it to ninety, hightailing it back to Codderville and civilization. I was hugging the inside lane when I saw the van moving up fast behind me. At almost level the entrance to the last turn off to Codderville, I cut the wheel ninety degrees and went sideways across the highway, bumping over dividers and grassy shoulder to get to the feeder road into town. The van kept going straight. The next exit wasn't for fifteen miles.

I pulled up in front of the Codderville Police Department, slammed on the brakes and killed the engine, jerking open the doors and grabbing the kids in one smooth move. We were inside before even they knew what had happened.

I told my story to three different uniforms in three different sittings at three different desks on three different occasions. On Saturday night in Codderville, Texas, nobody seemed to be in charge and none of the uniforms really seemed to care.

"Call Detective Luna," I said to anyone who'd listen. Which turned out to be nobody. Finally, I got up, went through the little half-door into the bullpen, and picked up a phone, dialing information for Elena Luna's home number. She answered on the first ring.

"Luna."

"Hi, it's E. J. Pugh."

"I'm so excited."

"My kids and I just got run off the road by somebody who must read the Codderville *News-Messenger*."

"Details."

So I gave them to her.

"Where are you?"

"At the police station, but nobody here seems to want to hear my story."

"I wonder why?" There was a sigh on the line. "Look. Stay. I'll be right there. Don't move."

I hung up and called my husband.

"Hello?"

"Willis?"

Silence.

"I know you're not speaking to me but you really don't have to. Just listen. A big van tried to run us off the road by hitting my car."

"Jesus! Honey, are you okay?"

"Well, I'm a little shook up."

"The kids?"

"They're okay. Nobody was hurt." I grinned. "Willis, remember *Bullitt?*"

89

There was a silence while he slid back in time. "Jesus, Eej . . ."

"Pure one-eighty. It was beautiful!"

He laughed. "Woman, what am I gonna do with you?"

"I'll tell you when I get home."

"I'm on my way now to pick you up."

"No, honey, the car's still drivable."

"No," he said, his Master of the Universe voice showing. "We'll change cars. Throw 'em off."

I nodded. "Okay. See you in a bit."

I went to the Group W Bench and sat down with my children, my arms around the girls, holding them tight. The excitement of the near miss would wear off soon, I knew, and reality would sink in. I could already feel the pride I'd felt in my perfect 180-degree turn begin to recede, replaced by pure panic. What a stupid thing to do! What if I'd messed it up? It's been eighteen years since I'd done a Bullitt and here I was putting not only my life and my children's lives in jeopardy, but the life of a very frightened, very traumatized little girl to boot.

*But what else could you have done?* the reasonable part of my brain argued.

*I don't know,* my panicky self answered.

*Run into the bridge abutment?* Reason asked.

*We could have been killed!* Panic answered.

*You did the right thing!* Reason insisted.

*Who were those guys and why did they do that to me?* Panic asked in a panicky, high-pitched squeal, not unlike that of a hog on its way to slaughter.

*They—he—it—was obviously the killer. You're on to something here, Eej,* Reason said.

*If I pack as soon as we get home, I could be at my mother's by midnight,* Panic said, sighing in relief.

*And put the rest of your family in jeopardy?* Reason reasoned.

It was just as Panic began to scream that the door

opened and Detective Elena Luna walked in, a brown paper bag with a grease stain on the bottom in one hand.

She walked up to the kids and knelt in front of them. "Hey, you must be Graham," she said. My son grunted in response. "And you're . . . ? looking at Megan.

Megan said, "Megan!" loudly.

Smiling, Luna moved on to Bessie. "And you're Bessie. Want a cookie?"

She pulled a giant chocolate-chip cookie out of her grease-stained paper bag. Bessie looked at me and I nodded my head. She took the cookie and watched as Megan and Graham got theirs. I wondered idly if any of Bessie's good manners might rub off on my two. Or would she just get as ornery as they in her quiet little way?

With the kids' attention consumed by chocolate chips and pecans, Luna turned to me.

"Woman." She shook her head.

"Just a coincidence, Luna?"

"You're gonna get yourself killed."

"Might happen. What with all these loose killers running amuck in our fair city."

The door to the outside opened, admitting wind, rain, and Willis Pugh. He ran up and hugged me.

"Baby, are you okay?"

I nodded and he headed for the kids, the two girls hugging him while Graham went into excruciating detail about the events of the evening.

Willis came back to where Luna and I stood and I introduced them. "Can't you do anything with your wife, Mr. Pugh? She needs a keeper, you know," Luna said.

Willis said, "Detective Luna, my wife has every right to do whatever is necessary to deal with the present situation. Since the police don't seem to be doing anything about it. I cannot and would not consider telling my wife what to do in this situation or any other."

Luna grinned and hit me on the arm. "Oooo, E.J., you

91

got a good one.'' With that, she left, into the bullpen to talk to some of the uniforms.

"What was that?" said Willis.

I shrugged. "Just girl talk. Don't worry your pretty little head about it."

"Very funny."

I kissed him full on the mouth. "You're a good man, Pugh."

" 'Bout goddamn time you noticed." Turning to the kids he said, "You guys ready?"

I called to Luna, "May I leave my car in your lot until tomorrow without getting a ticket?"

She waved me away. "Leave!" But she watched us all the way to the car.

We gathered the troops and headed for home, all of us except Bessie dissecting once again the events of the evening. Megan had thought the whole thing scary. Graham's opinion: "Excellent!" And Mom had been "bitchin'." He'd been reading his cousin's surfer mags again, obviously.

We got home, had a quick supper, and got the kids in bed. I'd noticed the minute I walked in my front door the mess in the living room. Wires and stuff all over the place and instructions for the installation of the burglar alarm system on the floor. I picked it all up and stuck it in a corner, out of harm's way but easily visible as a reminder to my husband.

Willis and I sat on the couch in the living room. "You still mad at me?" I asked.

"Funny how a near-death experience takes the sting outta being pissed." He put his arm around me and pulled me close. "I woulda missed you, babe," he said grinning.

"Yeah?" I grinned back. "How much?"

"Hell, a lot! I'd have to hire a maid to clean up and cook, then worry about carpooling with neighbors for the kids, and then, of course, all the extra expense of call girls on a weekly basis."

"Weekly?" I showed surprise. "How come they'd get it more than I do?"

He threw me down on the couch and straddled me. "Oh, now I understand! Is that the whole problem, ma'am? You ain't been getting enough?"

I giggled and squirmed under him. "Not in the living room!"

"They're asleep!" he said, his tongue going for one of my shell-like ears.

"Bessie," I said.

Willis sat up. Rubbed his face. Looked at me. "Bessie," he said.

"Sobering thought," I said, laying my head on his shoulder.

"What are we going to do?"

I shrugged. He took one of his huge hands and placed it under my chin, lifting my face to his. "Do you really think somebody could be after her?"

"It looks like it," I said.

Willis, pragmatic, practical, yet always one to put off anything disagreeable, got up and locked all the doors and windows, then came back and, throwing himself on the couch next to me, picked up the remote control and switched on the TV. It was ten-thirty, time to watch *Saturday Night Live*. Last week we'd sat in the same room watching the same program, a bottle of wine on the coffee table, the kids upstairs, Monique next door on the phone to one of her cronies, and Terry and Roy laughing at the Prime Time Players right along with us. We turned the show off halfway through without even discussing it and headed for bed.

# 9

I lay in bed thinking of things to come. Did we dare go to church tomorrow? None of our friends from church had even called since it all began. Did we walk in, towing an extra child and expect not to be stared at and whispered about? And why the hell did I feel guilty? Maybe it would be nice to sleep in on a Sunday.

And then I had to think about Monday. On Friday, during a lull, I'd called the cemetery to see if I could get plots next to Roy's and Terry's for the kids. They were delighted I'd called and explained they'd already put a reserve on the two plots adjoining the previously purchased ones. And then the asshole asked if I'd like to reserve a third for Bessie. Showing undue reserve for myself under any circumstances, I did not say, ''Fuck you, Jack,'' but let the gentleman know that would not be necessary. He told me I could come by Monday with a deposit check of $340. I told him I would, not mentioning that would be right after I went to the bank and withdrew the last of the savings and moved it into checking to cover all the rubbery checks I'd been writing.

Tuesday was reserved for the services. Maybe I should call Monday morning and make an appointment for that afternoon to see someone about how to deal with Bessie. Should she go to the funerals? If so, wouldn't I need to bring everything out beforehand? If she shouldn't go to the funerals, at what point did I bring up where her parents were? Where Aldon and Monique were? Why she couldn't go back to her house?

My sleep was fitful, but even so, when I awoke in the morning, Willis was just coming out of the shower; showered, shaved, and smelling good.

"You need to get up if we're going to church, babe," he said, hauling underwear out of his drawer.

"I don't want to go to church," I whined, rolling over and snuggling under the covers. I felt a pop on the rear end.

"You get up and get yourself decent. I'll start the kids."

I sat up in bed, saying, "Willis!" but he was already gone.

I got up with a feeling of dread. This wouldn't be the first time we'd gone to church without the Lesters. There'd been vacation times, sick times, don't-want-to-get-out-of-bed times, but it wasn't the same. No one there would wonder if the Lesters were sleeping in or on vacation. Everybody would know. And how would they react? Why hadn't anyone called?

I got out of bed and headed for the shower, standing under it longer than necessary, hoping time would run out and it would be too late to go. It didn't work that way. Willis had awakened everyone with plenty of time to spare. The asshole.

We drove the five blocks to the church. Sometimes we walked, when we were feeling very fifties and Americana, and all that stuff. More often than not, we drove.

The church parking lot was filling up fast as Willis pulled in and found a parking place under the shade of a giant oak. I sat in the car while Willis got the kids out. Finally, he came and opened my door.

"Sorry," he said. "Was I not being polite?"

"Huh?"

"I didn't open your door for you, so you're sitting in the car until I do?"

I laughed. "Honey, if I waited for that, arthritis would be setting in." I sighed. "I don't want to do this."

He took my hand. "I know. But we're going to."

We walked in like a family, heads high, little hands in big hands, Willis holding Megan's, Bessie's little hand in mine. Graham walked next to his father, his body language suggesting he was almost as tense as his mom.

The foyer outside the sanctuary was crowded, as it is every Sunday morning. People were talking, catching up on each other's weeks, making plans for church activities and social events in the week to come. As we entered, the room slowly started to hush, like a concert hall when the maestro comes into the orchestra pit; not all at once, but little by little until there was total silence. We were Moses and our church friends were the Red Sea parting silently before us as we walked into the sanctuary.

Behind us I could hear the conversations start up again; this time, though, I doubt if it had anything to do with church activities and social events.

Eyes in heads already seated in pews turned our way, then quickly turned back to hymnals, programs, anything to keep eyes off us. Rosemary Rush, already seated in the front row with her son, turned and saw us, gauged the reaction we were getting, and stood, walking up to us and hugging me lightly. Part of me knew Rosemary Rush always knew exactly the right thing to do and was big on doing it; another part of me was never so glad to see anyone in my life.

"Why don't ya'll come sit up front with Eric and me," she said, smiling, her arm hooked in mine, leading us to the front pew.

We sat, picking up our hymnals, studying the program, biding our time until the choir entered and Berry Rush started the day's sermon. I sat there, staring absently at the program, wondering why people were reacting in this way. *We* hadn't done anything wrong! When that thought entered my head, I wondered who it did imply had done something wrong. The Lesters? For getting killed? Shame on them! Part of me wanted to stand up and denounce everyone in the room for being the hypocritical bastards they were. And part of me knew if the shoe were on the other foot, maybe I too would be standing back, reticent, unable to put into words the mixed-up feelings such an event must bring.

Some of these people thought their friend—*our* friend—Roy Lester had murdered his family. Some might have doubts. Some had read the Saturday paper and assumed old E. J. Pugh was being her controversial self—always trying to shake things up, like wanting new playground equipment for the Sunday school yard. Some, the really small and petty ones, would not want their preschooler associating with Bessie, because of what her daddy might have done.

I sighed. They were just people, with all the fears and hatreds that people have. I felt a hand on my shoulder and turned in the pew to look behind me. Marilou Tanner sat in the second pew. She had chaired a committee I'd been on the year before. She and her husband Paul had been to a party at our house on New Year's Eve, and she and Roy had danced the limbo behind several Bloody Marys. They were our best friends at the church, next to the Lesters.

Marilou put her cheek to mine and whispered in my

ear, "We just heard. We've been out of town. What can I do?"

Tears welled up in my eyes and threatened to spill over. I touched the hand still on my shoulder. "Just be there," I said. She hugged me from the back while Paul shook hands with Willis, whispering something to him. Something positive I could tell, because Willis smiled and squeezed Paul's hand.

Ruby Gale Mason came up and knelt in front of me. Ruby Gale was the nursery supervisor and had known Megan and Bessie since they'd been in diapers. She patted my knee and took Bessie's hand in hers. "Hi, darlin', how you doing?" she whispered to Bessie. Bessie just looked at her, but then a small smile played across her face and she reached out and hugged Ruby Gale. Tears came to Ruby Gale's eyes as she hugged the child back. Patting my knee again, she said, "Let me know if there's anything I can do."

I smiled and nodded, not trusting myself to speak. Ruby Gale went back to her seat as the processional sounded and the choir began marching down the center aisle. Willis was sitting on the aisle seat, and I noticed several choir members pat his arm, squeeze his shoulder, and one elderly lady we barely knew pat him gently on the top of his head as they proceeded toward the choir loft.

Berry Rush's sermon was as boring as usual. Rosemary sat rigidly next to me, her spine a study in military correctness, while Eric fidgeted next to her. Eric was the ultimate end product of a union like that of Berry and Rosemary Rush's. Where the parents were stern, correct, earnest, and rigid, Eric was a nervous wreck.

He was a homely child of fourteen, his teeth in braces, his straw-colored hair cut as short as a first-year Marine's, and even so, it managed to have a cowlick. His face was matted with oozing acne, and he wore glasses so thick his eyes appeared huge and froglike behind them. Eric had no friends at the church and rarely spoke to anyone. The Rushes' older child, a daughter, we'd never met. The story I heard was that she was born severely mentally retarded and had been in a private care facility since birth. She was never mentioned much and I can't say that I've even heard her name. Knowing Rosemary and Berry, they might not have wasted a name on a severely mentally retarded child. At the home, she could be referred to as Rush One. I know, that's tacky, especially after what Rosemary had done for us today.

After the service, more people came up to us, some hugging, some merely shaking hands, others just smiling and nodding their sympathy. No one said anything directly, not in front of Bessie, and I was grateful for that.

On most Sundays, we'd leave the church and head for the buffet at the Claremont Motor Lodge out on the highway. Half the church was usually there. The two families, the Pughes and the Lesters, would pile in two cars and head for the highway. We'd get a large table and more often than not another family would join us. Terry and I always had a contest to see who could stick to just the salad bar. Usually we'd both lose, and pile our plates with fried chicken, ham, rare roast beef, potatoes au gratin, four different kinds of vegetables. We'd sit there sometimes until three in the afternoon, getting refills on our iced tea and gabbing.

This Sunday we went straight home to BLTs and the Sunday baseball game. I sat in the living room with Willis and Graham, pretending to watch the game. Instead I was worrying. What had I not done? Did I order flowers? Oh, right. No flowers. Contributions instead. I needed to do that. Here I'd been telling everybody else to, and I hadn't sent a penny to the Codderville Children's Foundation. Not that I actually had a penny to send. Had to go to the bank tomorrow. Then to the cemetery office. Had to see Reverend Rush at some point. Check out his sermon. Oh, shit. A eulogy. Someone should give a eulogy. I looked at Willis. He was the most obvious choice. Would he do it? He'd given a eulogy at Rusty's funeral and it almost killed him. I needed to make a list. Lots of lists. I needed to organize this thing before it got totally away from me.

I got up and grabbed my purse and slipped on my shoes.

"Where you going?" Willis asked, his face actually turned from the TV set.

"Have to go into town. I need something at the office supply store."

"Can't it wait until tomorrow?"

I shook my head. "I have entirely too much to do tomorrow. I'll be back in a minute. The girls are upstairs."

"You okay?" Willis asked.

I smiled. "Yeah, honey, I'm okay."

I waved and headed out the door. I'd blocked the previous day's experience from my mind. Until I got on the highway into Codderville. My body reacted before my mind did. My mind, bless its heart, was under some undue pressure. My hands began to shake so hard I could barely hold the steering wheel, while my eyes were darting back and forth from rearview mirror to side mirrors, looking, I suppose, for black vans. None were found. I took the first exit into Codderville and pulled into a service station, stopping the engine and sitting for a moment. The station was closed on Sunday, so nobody came running out to help me or shoo me away. Someone had tried to kill me yesterday. Me and the kids. Someone wanted us dead. Or someone wanted Bessie dead. And I had started that. Me. With my big mouth. I had set the wheels into motion that could cause the demise of Terry's only surviving child, and my kids and me to boot.

Somebody had killed the Lesters. Murdered them. If I'd had any doubt before, if somewhere in my being a nagging atom wanted to blame Roy for the deaths, it was gone now. I was convinced. The black van was no coincidence. Definitely no accident. I hadn't cut any one off, hadn't stolen a parking space, hadn't been driving too fast, too slow, or over the line. I hadn't committed any violations that would inflame a motorist to mayhem. It had been deliberate. Attempted murder. But the police didn't think so. Even if they did, even if I could convince Elena Luna that someone was out to get Bessie, I hadn't gotten a license number. There was no way to trace the black van. I wasn't even sure of the make and model. It could have been Japanese or domestic. It wasn't a Volkswagen van, of that I was sure. But that was all I was sure of. Except that someone had tried to kill us.

I shuddered and looked around. Here I was at an empty gas station right off the exit ramp of the highway, right next to the access road. There were no other businesses on that side of the highway. To get to Codderville, you had to go up a block, under the highway overpass, and then into town. I sat here. In a different car from that of the day before, but still— . . . I started the engine and got the hell out of there.

The office supply place was open. I went in and looked at the binders and pads and forms. I wanted something to organize my pain. Put it in neat little piles. After ten minutes of looking I found it. The Office Organizer. It was eight and a half by eleven inches, had a brown Leatherette binding and, when you opened it up, on one side, up in the corner, were "WHILE YOU WERE OUT" slips for messages, right next to a "THINGS TO DO" pad. Under these was a Leatherette sleeve for catching loose pieces of paper—like receipts and bills. On the other side were two five-by-six-inch yellow-lined notepads. Under these was an address book and, next to that, a five-year calendar. It cost $13.95

and was worth twice that much to me. It would make everything better. I knew that. In my heart and in my soul.

Next door to the office supply house was a children's shop. In the window was a display of *101 Dalmatians*. Well, maybe not 101, but there were a bunch of stuffed, black-spotted white puppies. I went in to get one for Bessie. As I was checking out, the mother guilt got to me. I went back and bought another for Megan and found some Ninja Turtle figures Graham didn't already possess. I bought those too, which brought the hot check I was writing that day up to $37.10. Add that to the hot check I'd just written to the office supply place and that amounted to a considerable amount of money in the last few days I'd spent with little to back it up.

Sitting in the car, I took my Office Organizer out of the sack and opened it. Taking the pen that was in its own little ring on the inside of the binder, I wrote on the THINGS TO DO pad item number one, "Go to bank to transfer funds." I closed it and set it on the seat next to me, feeling righteous.

# 10

Once at home, sitting at the kitchen table, I filled in two and a half pages of "THINGS TO DO" before I made myself stop. When I realized I'd written down "Try to become a better person," I felt it was possible I was obsessing.

We usually spent Sunday evening at Willis' mother's house. Not that I'd ever been asked if that was a way I'd like to spend my Sunday evenings. It's just what we'd done since moving to Codderville four years before. Every goddamn Sunday night for four years. We'd sit in the living room and talk. Then she'd jump up and run into the kitchen for something, making me feel that I'd better do that too if I wanted to wear the title "woman."

What we usually did in the kitchen was check through the kitchen windows to make sure her dogs were okay, check to make sure the refrigerator was running, check to make sure the oven wasn't on, check to make sure the iron wasn't plugged in, check to make sure the kitchen was still there and hadn't flooded in her ten-minute absence. We rarely spoke on these kitchen excursions, she and I. It was just something good Pugh women did.

I looked up from my list to the kitchen clock. It was ten to six. I needed to fix the kids a light supper before we headed for Grandma's. I wondered how Grandma was going to take to her new granddaughter. I moved into the living room where the ball game was winding down.

"You want me to fix you something to eat when I fix the kids'?" I asked Willis.

"Um? What time is it?"

"Ten to six."

"I'd better call Mama," he said, reaching for the phone.

"Why?"

"To let her know we're not coming."

"Why? Why aren't we going?"

"Well, honey, under the circum—"

"Willis. Jesus. Don't you think life's screwed up enough for the kids? We always go to Grandma's on Sunday nights! *Always!* There is no reason to change that now!"

Willis looked at me. Whether at my vehemence or just the fact that I actually was arguing to *go* to his mother's, I'm not sure. Finally, he said, "Well, okay. I guess you're right."

"Do you want me to fix you something to eat?"

"What are you fixing the kids?"

"Soup."

"What kind?"

I put my hands on my hips to keep them from going around his neck. "What kind do you want?"

"Do we have any of that noddle stuff that takes longer than the canned kind?"

"Yes."

"Do we have time for you to fix that?"

106

"Yes." I turned and headed into the kitchen to fix the noodle stuff.

We were on the road by a quarter till seven, each child buckled in the back seat with a new toy. Bessie hugged her dalmatian, kissed him, and had him kiss Ernie, who came along for the ride.

"On the way home, we need to stop by the police station and pick up the wagon," Willis said.

I nodded. I wasn't thrilled about that. Maybe it wouldn't start, I thought. Maybe the front fender was bent too far in and would scrape against the tire. One could only hope.

Mrs. Pugh met us on the porch. We were approximately three minutes later than usual. She worried. She said that. A lot. It was her litany. "I worry."

The kids piled out of the car, Bessie taking up the rear. Mrs. Pugh had met Bessie before, of course. She'd often sat for the four little ones when Monique had other plans and couldn't. Mrs. Pugh hugged Megan and Graham and then turned her attention to Bessie.

"Well, Miss Bessie. How are you?" she said, bending her arthritic back down to the child's height.

Bessie looked at her and smiled tentatively.

"You remember me?" Mrs. Pugh asked. Bessie nodded. "Well, you come on in here," Mrs. Pugh said, holding out a hand to Bessie. Bessie took it and followed her inside the house. "You've never been to my house, have you? I've always seen you at Megan and Graham's house. Did you know I have three dogs?" Bessie shook her head. "Well, I surely do. And they're all out back and just jumping for joy to know there's a new little girl come to play." She turned to her grandson. "Graham, you take the girls out in the back to meet the dogs and you make sure them dogs don't jump all over Bessie's pretty little dress. You understand me?"

"Yes, ma'am," Graham said, leading the girls outside.

That's another thing. Graham's never said "yes, ma'am" to me in his entire life!

We three, the adults, stood in the living room and watched the children walk through the kitchen and out the back door. Once they were out the door, Mrs. Pugh waved us to the sofa. Sitting herself down in her straight-backed armchair, she said, "Well?"

Willis and I looked at each other.

Mrs. Pugh sighed. "Is she okay?"

I took that one. "Yes, ma'am," I said, just as dutiful as my seven-year-old. "Physically, she's fine. She hasn't spoken yet, though. The doctors don't know when she will."

"Well," Mrs. Pugh said, her back rigid and her hands steady on the arms of the chair, "I don't hold with psychiatric stuff generally, but I think this is one of them cases where that's what should be done. Get her to a psychiatrist." She sniffed. "Of course, that's just my opinion."

I nodded my head. "I agree. I'm going to call someone tomorrow to talk to them about whether or not Bessie should go to the funeral service."

Again, Mrs. Pugh sniffed. "I don't hold with children going to funerals. It's not right. Not a place for children."

I nodded my head but didn't say anything.

"Of course, under these circumstances, you'd best ask one of them people."

"I thought I'd do that."

"What about the house?"

"Ma'am?"

"You cleaned it yet?"

Inwardly, I shuddered at the thought. "No, ma'am, not yet."

"Well, blood sets up pretty fast. Probably already ruint them carpets and things."

"I thought I'd call a cleaning service after the funerals.'' Something to add to my THINGS TO DO list. I could always scratch out "become a better person."

Mrs. Pugh snorted. Her imitation of a laugh. "Won't find nobody in this town to do that. People feel washing blood out's a personal thing."

"Well, I thought I'd just call around."

"Won't find nobody."

I nodded. Willis changed the subject.

"Heard from Juney?"

Mrs. Pugh sniffed. My only redeeming quality in her eyes is that I wasn't her other daughter-in-law, Juney. Juney and Rusty were married three weeks before he was killed. Two weeks after, we found out she was pregnant. As Juney was a throwaway (her mother and stepfather had tossed her out when she was fifteen), she stayed with Mrs. Pugh during the pregnancy. Immediately after the birth, Juney took off, leaving the newborn baby boy with his grandmother, which was just peachy keen with Grandma. On Garth's first birthday, Juney showed up with a new husband and a new bun in the oven and demanded her son back. That was a year ago. We haven't heard from her since, but Willis keeps asking, usually when his mother is aiming her arrows at me.

"Not a word. The ungrateful thing. I saw her mama in the store the other day, though, and she said she thinks she's living in Tyler. Can you imagine—saying *you think* maybe you know where your child is! Disgraceful!"

I agreed, inwardly and verbally. Juney never had a chance and she knew it. The night Rusty died, the two of them had had a fight at a bar in town. Rusty was drunk and took off in his pickup truck. Going over eighty miles an hour, he hit a tree. There weren't any skid marks. According to Mrs. Pugh, if Juney had been a proper wife, she and her husband would have been home in their trailer where they belonged, not out at some bar. And she never would have fought with him in public—if she'd been a proper wife. Therefore, Rusty would not have died. End of discussion.

Mrs. Pugh never said these things directly to Juney. Although she did say them in her presence. To other people. Mrs. Pugh didn't believe in direct conflict. Personally, I thought Juney was a whiny, self-indulgent little shit, but she didn't deserve the seven months of hell Mrs. Pugh put her through during her pregnancy. But, of course, that's just my opinion.

"You want coffee?" Mrs. Pugh asked.

Willis shrugged, but his mother wasn't looking anyway, so it didn't matter. When at Mrs. Pugh's, one drank her coffee. End of discussion. I followed her into the kitchen to help, because that's what I was supposed to do.

As she filled the cups I looked out the window into the back yard. Graham and Megan were running, playing chase with the poodle and the dachshund. The cocker spaniel, Winston, lay in Bessie's lap where she sat under a mulberry tree. Dalmation and Ernie sat on the ground, discarded while Bessie showered all her affection on Winston. Something new to add to my "THINGS TO DO" list. Buy the kids a damned dog. And be quick about it.

"How you holding up?" Mrs. Pugh asked, taking me completely by surprise. She'd never actually asked me a personal question, to my recollection.

"Uh, okay."

"You're a good mother. Your friend made a wise decision leaving that baby to you."

With that, she walked out of the kitchen, into the living room, leaving me in utter bewilderment.

I walked in and sat down next to my husband, picking up my coffee cup and sipping, trying to hide my shock. There had been too damn many changes in my life in less than a week. I certainly didn't need my mother-in-law turning into a human being to confuse me further.

When darkness fell completely, I called the kids inside.

110

For the rest of the evening, Graham and Megan played and argued in "their" bedroom, the one they stayed in when they spent the night. Bessie sat by the glass storm door, Winston the cocker spaniel on the other side, his nose touching the glass. Bessie's fingers stroked the glass where Winston's nose touched.

We left and went the two blocks out of our way to pick up the wagon. The plan was: Willis would keep the kids in his car and I would drive the wagon home, him following me in case it broke down. Or anything. I got in, put the key in the ignition, and started the engine. It turned over. Great, I thought, sighing. I pulled out of the parking lot, hoping for the sound of metal screeching against tire. It didn't come. Actually, the car ran perfectly. Probably needed new tires because of the beating my perfect 180 did to them, but other than that, it seemed okay. The drive home was nerve-racking. But there were no signs of black vans or any other malevolent vehicles. I pulled into the driveway unharmed.

We had the kids in bed by nine-thirty. I took my bath and, before crawling into bed, took my tour of the house, something I'd been doing every night since it happened, even after Willis locked up. He could miss a window. Forget a door. Not turn on a nightlight downstairs. Finding everything on the ground floor secure, I went upstairs, checked Graham to make sure he was still breathing, and checked his windows to make sure they were locked. Then I went into the girls' room. Both little chests were moving in a pattern consistent with life. I went on to check the windows.

A light was burning in the Lester house.

My stomach heaved, my palms went clammy, and the skin over my entire body tightened. A car pulling out of a driveway across the street turned, its lights no longer reflecting off the downstairs front window. It moved on and the Lester house became dark again. My body, how-

111

ever, didn't want to give up its claim to fright. I stood there, staring at the dark sentry that had once been a happy, well-lit, noise-filled space. It just stood there with its secret, silent as Bessie. I shuddered and left the room, crawling quickly under the covers that had saved me so many times as a child.

I lay there as Willis took his shower, wondering when I'd stop waking up with that feeling of unknown dread. When I'd remember not to save newspaper clippings and juicy gossip for Terry. When Bessie would speak again.

I rolled over on my side so the tears I was shedding would stay out of my ears. One of the problems of crying in bed.

By the time Willis crawled in next to me, I was dry-eyed and ready for serious talk.

"We need to buy the kids a dog."

He looked at me.

"Really," I said.

He looked away.

"Willis, did you hear me?"

He sighed. "I heard you. I don't want a dog."

"Why?"

"It's too much responsibility."

I almost laughed. Three kids, two mortgages, and a business, and he called a dog too much responsibility.

"The kids will take care of it."

"Ha."

"I'll make sure they do."

"Who's going to pay the vet bills when they pull it's damn legs off learning to share?"

I sighed. He'd hit a reasonable possibility there. One dog with three kids, two of them being Megan and Graham, the "it's mine" twins, could lead to problems. Three dogs? Goldfish? Kittens!

"Okay, we'll get three kittens."

"What!"

"Cats take care of themselves. They shit and cover it up. They wash themselves. That would be perfect."

Willis crawled under the covers, flicking off his bedside lamp. "I'm allergic to cats," he said, his back to me.

I pulled him over to face me. "No, you're not. You just don't like cats."

"Same thing."

"No, it's not."

Willis sat up. "Why this sudden desire for animals, Eej?"

"You didn't see Bessie tonight."

"Sure I did."

"At your mother's. Out in the back yard, she put down that damned Ernie doll for the first time since she's been home. You know why? To cuddle Winston, that's why. A real live thing. Even after I brought the kids in the house, she stayed right by the back door, communicating with that damned dog."

"I never did like Winston," Willis said.

I sat up and pulled his face towards me, two fingers squeezing his mouth into an O shape. "Listen to me, Willis Stephenson Pugh. There is such a thing as pet therapy. I've read about it. It will be good for Bessie to have a pet. Something of her own. But you're right, we can't have one pet for three kids. So we'll get three pets. You will have to learn to live with it. Do you understand me?"

He gently removed my fingers from his mouth. "If I step in cat shit once—*once*, E.J.—we'll be having fricasseed pussy for dinner, you understand?"

"Oooo, Willis, you animal!" I giggled.

He pressed me down on the bed. "I'm not kidding."

I moaned in exaggerated ecstasy. "You know talking about torturing small animals gets me hot."

"You're a sick woman," Willis said, nuzzling my neck. "I've always found that attractive."

# 11

Monday was a booger-bear. I dropped Graham off at the grammar school, Megan off at the Montessori, and drove into Codderville, where I dropped Bessie off at Mrs. Pugh's for the day. Then I went back to Black Cat Ridge to the bank and transferred funds from our savings (the last of it, keeping $25 in place to hold the account open) to our checking. Then I drove back into Codderville to the Memorial Hill Cemetery, where I met Mr. Simpson, the salesman for the cemetery. How'd you like that as a job? I mean, they say a good salesman can sell anything and I have a brother-in-law who is one. He's sold oilfield supplies, oil leases and real estate, and is currently the district manager for a company that makes screws. But could he transfer right into selling cemetery plots? Why not? It's just small real estate, I guess. I wrote out the check for the deposit and left as quickly as possible. He said everything would be ready at three the next afternoon.

I found a pay phone at a 7-Eleven and called Marilou Tanner from the church. She'd had a child molested five years before. I figured she'd be a good contact for a therapist for Bessie.

"Hello?"

"Marilou, this is E.J."

"Oh, honey, how are you?"

"Okay. Look, I'm at a pay phone so I can't really talk." The main reason I didn't call her from the house. "I need the name of a therapist for Bessie. I need to see someone today. I thought maybe . . ."

"Sure. Tommy saw a woman in Codderville named Elaine Comstock. An MSW."

"What's that?"

"Stands for master's in social work."

"She's a social worker?"

"Well, no, actually, she's a certified psychotherapist. But her degree is an MSW."

"She's good?"

"Excellent. Worked with Tommy for two years and with Paul and me. Even had Brad"—their other son—"in a few times. Worked with the whole family."

"Well, I guess that's what we're going to need."

"I think so, honey. Look, E.J." She sighed. "It's not easy. But I guess none of this is going to be easy."

"No. I guess not." I sighed my own sigh. "Thanks, Marilou. I've got to run."

"Keep me posted."

"I will. Bye."

I hung up and dialed information, getting the number of Elaine Comstock. I dialed.

"Family Center."

"Uh, I need to make an appointment with Elaine Comstock for today. It's sort of an emergency."

"I'm sorry, Ms. Comstock doesn't have any openings today. May I tell her what this is concerning?"

116

Briefly, I told the receptionist the problem. "Okay, Mrs. Pugh. Look. I've got fifteen minutes I can squeeze you into. That way you can get some quick advice about the funerals and set up for a session with the child for later. How does that sound?"

"Wonderful."

"Can you be here in ten minutes?"

"Where are you located?"

She gave me an address less than five minutes away. "I'll be there," I said, and hung up.

Elaine Comstock was a five-foot-seven-inch blue-eyed blonde. She definitely wasn't toothpaste-commercial pretty, but she had a face full of intelligence and strength. I liked her immediately. We went into her office and sat.

"Usually, I like to give my clients a little breathing space, but I don't think we have time for that," she said with a smile.

"I understand, and I really appreciate your seeing me on such short notice."

"Dorothy said you're burying the child's family tomorrow."

"Yes. I'm not sure at this point if Bessie even knows they're dead. She can't speak, as I said, so I have no idea what she knows or thinks or feels."

"I wouldn't be surprised if she's suffering a little amnesia right now. A form of blocking. Usually, if a child is old enough, I feel they should go to the funerals of their loved ones. It's a closure, a way of saying good-bye. But under these circumstances, I'd say no. Wait. The lack of speech is a fairly serious development. I'd like to work on that a while, letting her tell us finally what's going on. Do you understand?"

I nodded my head.

"Later, when she's ready, she can go to the cemetery. Have her own good-bye ceremony. With her new family."

Again, I nodded my head.

"How are your other children handling her?"

I shook my head. "I think Megan's mad because Bessie won't speak, but she won't say anything to me because I told her not to be. Dumb, huh?"

Elaine smiled. "Not dumb. Ill-informed. Megan is probably not reacting to Bessie as she normally would, and that is probably not helping Bessie. I understand your wanting Megan to be sensitive to Bessie's needs, but a four-year-old is not necessarily capable of that kind of compassion without getting a little miffed."

Light dawned. Megan wasn't an unusually rotten child. She was normal!

Elaine stood up and I followed her out to the reception desk. "Dorothy, set Bessie up for a play session as soon as possible." To me, she said, "I'd like to set one up with Megan, too. These two are very connected from what you tell me. They've been best friends forever and now they're sharing a room. They're going to be sisters. We need to make sure now there aren't any hidden problems that could backfire later."

I nodded my head. I didn't want to ask, but I had to. "How much?"

"Seventy-five dollars an hour." Elaine smiled. "But most insurance companies pay for it now. Check with yours." She put her hand on my arm and squeezed. "There's no charge for today, of course. And we'll defer any payments over the insurance coverage until after the estate is through probate."

I almost burst into tears. "Thanks," I managed to get out.

"Dorothy will give you the times for Bessie and Megan's play sessions. Good luck."

With that she was gone, finding another patient in the waiting room to take back to her inner sanctum. Dorothy handed me a card with the two appointments written down and smiled. "We'll see you then, Mrs. Pugh. And my condolences."

I nodded, smiled and left. Every once in a blue moon my estimation of the human condition has to be slightly reevaluated to fit in the fact that there are nice people in this world.

I found another pay phone and called the church office, getting Berry Rush.

"Reverend Rush," he said.

"Hi, this is E.J."

"Hello, E.J. How are you holding up, dear? I was happy to see how the congregation rallied round yesterday."

"Fine. I'm fine. And yes, they were wonderful. Look, I'm at a pay phone. I need to see your sermon before tomorrow."

"I beg your pardon?"

"I'll be by in a few minutes to get a copy. Bye." I hung up. I had my reasons. I didn't want any reference made to the erroneous assumption that Roy Lester had killed his family. I didn't feel I could trust Berry Rush not to do that. I stopped by the church on the way home and walked into Reverend Rush's office. He stood up upon seeing me, his hands outstretched. I shook one briefly.

"Do you have that copy for me?"

"E.J., please, sit down," he said, expansively waving toward a chair.

I shook my head. "I really don't have time. I have a million things to do. Do you have that copy?"

"E.J., you must admit that's a rather unusual request. I don't believe in my twenty-one years of serving the Lord I have ever been asked by a member of my congregation to view any sermon I'm to give. Wedding vows some couples feel are open to interpretation, but of course, you know I don't allow that in weddings I perform. I certainly don't feel I need a critique on a sermon for a funeral. Even

119

the most liberal of the clergy don't allow their sermons to be rewritten by members of their congregation."

Nothing to it but to do it. I sat down. "Berry," I said, too tired to play the little games he liked so well, "let's cut to the chase."

His response was total silence. I don't think that's ever happened before.

I continued. "I don't want any references at all to the general assumption that Roy killed his family. He didn't and it will soon be proven he didn't and I don't want the family going to their final reward with gossip and innuendo at their goddamn funeral."

"I see."

"I have no idea, of course, what you intended to say at the service. But I'd prefer it if you kept it to mostly religious readings and short personal remembrances. Willis has agreed to do the eulogy. At what point do you feel that should occur?"

"I'll discuss that with Willis."

"When?"

"Tomorrow, right before the service." He stood up. "If that's all, E.J. . . ."

Dismissal is a nasty thing, but I was ready to leave anyway. "You understand about the sermon, Reverend Rush?"

"I had no intention of saying what a naughty boy Roy was for killing his family, E.J."

I sighed. Jesus, I'd hurt his feelings. "I know that. I'm sorry if I've offended you. It's just that I don't want any references made to that . . ."

He nodded. "I understand. Good day."

He sat back down at his desk, his head bent toward the papers spread before him. Well, I wouldn't be winning any Sunday school Member of the Year awards, that's for sure.

I left for home and the eulogy I'd promised to write for

Willis. I went to my office under the stairs, brought up the computer file, and sat there staring at the blank screen. I keyed in "Eulogy." And sat and stared at that. Then I turned it off and went to gather up recyclables for pickup on Tuesday.

It was while I was gathering the newspaper that I noticed it. On the same page with the report that had so pissed me off that I'd gone to the *News-Messenger* office and set the wheels in motion that almost got me killed. But there it was. Right on the front page. Along with the article about the high school counselor getting killed in a car wreck. The headline, CODDER COUNTY UTILITY COMMISSIONERS UNDER INVESTIGATION. Shenanigans at the County Utility. At which friend Roy had been manager. I read the article.

"The Commissioners of the Codder County Utility are under investigation for misappropriations of funds. County Attorney Edward Jones' office told this News-Messenger reporter that, although they are looking into rumors, nothing concrete has been proved yet. Jones also states that the suicide of Utility Director Roy Lester does not appear to be connected."

That was it. Absolutely nothing. Which the *News-Messenger* seemed to be very good at. But I did wonder why Ed Jones figured there was no connection between that and Roy's "suicide." I wondered about that very much.

I picked up the phone and dialed the Codderville Police Department, asking to speak to Detective Luna. When I was asked who was calling, I almost didn't give out my name, afraid Luna wouldn't come to the phone if she knew it was me.

Less than a minute later my fears were proved false.

"What now?" came the slightly Hispanic accent.

"Greetings to you too, good friend Luna."

"We're not buddies, Pugh, so cut the shit. What do you want?"

"My, aren't we hostile today?"

A long-suffering sigh escaped through the phone wires. Enough already, I thought.

"Did you see the article in last week's *News-Messenger* about hanky-panky at the Utility Commission?"

"Yeah. So?"

"So. Roy Lester was manager of the Utility Commission."

"Yeah. I repeat, so?"

I let out my own long-suffering sigh. "Elena, come on. There could be a connection."

"That's like saying he's white so it's a race thing. Or he's male, so it must have been militant feminists."

"No, it's not. He was the *only* director at the *only* utility commission in the county. That narrows it down a bit more than being male and white."

"Okay," Luna said, "how's this for a scenario? As manager, Roy Lester was piddling with the books, was going to get caught, and decided to end it all and save his family from the humiliation."

"As a scenario? Pretty stupid. How's this? One—or all—of the commissioners had something going. Scamming the books, whatever. Roy found out about it and they, the commissioners, conspired to have him killed, and his whole family was wiped out to make it look like a murder-suicide."

"E.J., give it up."

"It's a better scenario than yours!"

"E.J., go away."

"Look. Somebody killed the Lester family. You know it and I know it. It wasn't a murder-suicide. That's a given—"

"Not to me—"

"*And* somebody tried to run me off the road when I had Bessie—the only witness—in the car with me. Now what does that mean?"

"It means there are some bad drivers out during storms. They come out from under rocks. *That's* a given!"

For the first time since I'd met Detective Elena Luna, I was getting a sinking, helpless feeling. "You're really not going to help me, are you?" I asked her, quietly.

"Look, E.J." There was a long silence. "My hands are tied."

"Sounds self-inflicted to me."

She sighed. "If you ever, I mean *ever,* come up with something concrete, call me."

She hung up and I sat there staring at the receiver in my hand.

I had an hour before I needed to pick up the kids, starting with Bessie at Grandma's house in Codderville. I went to the window and looked out at the lawn. Clouds were gathering to the east, big black nasty-looking ones. Another spring storm. Around here you could never tell what those clouds were carrying. Rain with lightning and thunder. Or hail. Or tornadoes. Always a surprise. I looked past the lawn to the Lester house next door, sitting forlorn and abandoned. I hadn't been in there since Friday morning, when I'd gone to get Bessie's stuff. I should check on it, I thought. Make sure everything's okay. Somewhere, deep in my being, I knew that wasn't the real reason. The house compelled me. Beckoned me. I stepped out my back door and crossed the side-by-side driveways, large drops of rain pelting my head and shoulders, to the back door of the Lester house. Using my key, I unlocked it, stepping inside the dark kitchen. My foot hit something grainy and I almost slipped, grabbing the kitchen table for support. I flipped on the light switch. The kitchen had been ransacked. Totally trashed. All the cupboard doors stood open, plates and glasses smashed on the floor, staples and condiments—the only foodstuffs still there after I'd cleaned up on Friday—smeared the counters, floor, and tabletops.

I stood still and listened. Not a sound. No one could be repeating this performance in other parts of the house without making quite a racket. A week ago I would have run like a jackrabbit on seeing this kind of mess. But I was tired of running and being afraid. What I was now was pissed. That somebody could do this with me right next door. When had it happened? In the middle of the night, while we slept? Luna wanted something concrete? Well, by God, this was pretty damned concrete!

I went to the wall phone in the kitchen and dialed Luna for the second time in an hour.

"What?" she said, her voice clipping dangerously at the *t*.

"You want concrete?"

"What's happened?"

"I'm at the Lester's house. It's been trashed. Totaled. You wanna come have a look?" I hung up the phone, almost grinning in my triumph.

# 12

"A cut-and-dried burglary," Luna said.

"Shit!" I threw up my hands in disgust. Looking around the living room, I said, "You call yourself a detective? A three-year-old could tell this place's been searched!"

She glanced around at the knife-torn couches and chairs, upended with the bottoms also slashed; the potted plants uprooted and all the dirt poured out on the floor; the paintings ripped off the walls, their canvases slashed; the carpet ripped up at the corners and pulled to the center of the room. This was no "cut-and-dried burglary."

"Every room's like this," I told her.

"You've gone through the whole house?"

I sighed. "I had a while to wait for you, you know."

"Thought maybe you'd prove your point?" Luna looked at me. I didn't like the look she was giving me.

"What?"

"I said not to call unless you had something concrete.

Maybe you decided to manufacture something you considered concrete.''

''Jesus Christ!'' My hands were on my hips and the look on my face must have matched hers in intensity.

Luna broke eye contact by taking out a small notebook from her purse. ''Okay, when was the last time you were in here?''

''Before I started tearing the place up?'' I asked.

She looked up from the notebook. ''When was the last time you were in the house before today?''

''Friday morning. I came over to get Bessie's stuff so she could leave the hospital.''

''Everything was okay then?''

I nodded my head. ''I cleaned out the refrigerator and took out the trash.''

''So sometime between Friday—when?''

''Midmorning. Around nine or ten.''

''Okay, so sometime between then and now somebody broke in here and burglarized the place. Can you tell what's missing?''

I pointed at the almost brand-new twenty-two-inch Sony TV in the living room. ''Seems funny to me they'd smash a thousand-dollar TV rather than take it, doesn't it to you?''

''Did they have VCRs?''

I nodded. ''Yeah. Two.''

''Where were they?''

''One here,'' I pointed to the empty space on the stand under the TV, ''and one upstairs with the other TV.''

Luna shrugged, her body posture saying, Enough said.

''So what if they took two VCRs? Together brand-new they weren't worth a thousand dollars!''

''Easier to carry than that huge TV. Smash-and-grab types.''

''Who systematically searched the whole house?'' I whirled around, pointing at the destruction. ''This isn't

126

smash-and-grab, Luna! So they took a couple of things to make it look like a burglary! Jesus, how stupid are you?"

Boy, had I gone too far. Luna turned and looked at me and I wished I was anywhere but in the Lesters' living room at that moment. "Not stupid enough to make myself a sitting duck for God knows what. Not stupid enough to put Bessie and my own kids in jeopardy by blabbing to the newspapers. And not stupid enough to try to alienate the only people on my side."

"Are you on my side?" I asked. "How the hell can I tell that? By all the tremendous support?"

"By the fact that you're not in a jail cell for obstructing justice!" Luna turned away from me for a moment, then turned back, grabbing my arm and marching me towards the kitchen.

"You can't arrest me!" I screamed. "I haven't done anything!"

There was no response as she marched me out the back door and across the driveways to my own back door.

"House arrest? Can you do that?" I asked, my voice rising in indignation and something akin to fear for my freedom.

She marched me into my own living room and practically threw me, if she'd been big enough, onto the couch.

"Who in the hell do you think—" I started.

"Shut up." Luna stood there looking at me. Finally, she rubbed dark hair out of her face, put her hands on her hips, and surveyed the living room. "E.J. Listen." She turned back to me. "Something's going on. I know it and you know it—"

I sat up straight. "Then why—"

"Shut up! For once in your goddamn life let somebody else talk! Okay?"

I slouched back on the couch. "Okay. But—"

"Enough! Listen. I've been talking with Ed Jones." My ears pricked up. Okay, now we're getting somewhere, I thought. "This thing at the Utility Commission is big, E.J. Very big. It could involve some very important people. Ed is playing it very low-key. Whether or not Roy was involved, he won't say. But he and his people are on it. They'll find out what happened. Meanwhile, you're out here playing in the dark, making people think you know things that you don't know! You can get yourself killed and you've definitely put Bessie in jeopardy! Do you understand that?"

"You don't think Roy did it, do you?"

Luna sighed. "I don't know."

I stood up. "I have to go pick up the kids."

"I'll drive you."

"You don't have to do that—"

"Shut up and get in the car." She walked towards the back door, heading for the driveway, where her cruiser was parked.

"You know, I'm getting really tired of you telling me to shut up," I said to her back, following.

"Get in the car."

"Yes, sir."

"Shut up, Pugh."

Typical of a Texas spring, the rain that had spotted my clothing and the dark clouds that had threatened worse were gone. The sun was shining and the sky cloudless. I got in the car and shut up until Luna asked for directions, which I grudgingly gave. After we had Megan and Graham in the cruiser, each asking for Luna to run the siren, talk on the radio, turn on the lights, etc., we headed for Codderville to pick up Bessie. After she was in the car, I said, "No reason for you to drive us all the way back to Black Cat Ridge. Why don't you just drop us off at Willis' office? We'll ride back with him."

She nodded and headed towards the highway where the two-story office building that housed Willis' three-room suite was located. I herded the kids out of the car

128

and was turning to leave when Luna said, "E.J., listen."

"What?"

"I'm sorry if I got rough with you."

I shrugged.

"I'm scared for you and the kids."

"We'll be okay."

"Maybe. If you're full of shit. Unfortunately, if you're not, if you're right, things could go bad."

I leaned against the car. "Maybe I am full of shit," I said, wondering for the first time if that could be true. If Roy really did do everything everybody said he did and if I was just playing wishing games. Wishing my friend hadn't been a homicidal maniac.

Luna reached through the car window and squeezed my arm. "Call me. Anytime of the day or night." She took out a card and scribbled her home phone number on the back. Handing it to me, she said, "Be careful."

I took the card. "Yeah. More careful than I have been. You're right. I've been stupid."

Luna grinned. "Yeah, well, civilians sometimes think life is a made-for-TV movie." The grin faded. "It's not."

She put the car in gear and pulled away. I gathered the kids and went into the building.

The Oak Hills Office Tower was built on what used to be a hill covered in oaks. When they decided to build something there, they bulldozed the oaks and flattened the top of the hill. And, since it was only two stories tall, it wasn't much of a tower, either, but developers have their dreams and who am I to bombard them with semantics? It was a typical two-year-old building. A large, open lobby with lots of plants reaching up to skylights in the ceiling. The offices were in a square around the open lobby. There was an elevator for the fat and lazy and an open staircase for the swift of foot. We took the elevator.

Willis had a three-room suite: a small reception room where his part-time secretary, Rosie Morales, typed up letters, filed, and greeted, a small office where Willis met with clients, and a large room with drafting tables, computers, layout boards, and a coffee bar where the actual work was done. Willis had two free-lance drafters who worked with him on large projects, when they were in town and not off somewhere trying to make a living. Only one was here now, Ricky Heimer, a twenty-three-year-old, fresh out of drafting school, tall, skinny, acne-scarred, with a protruding Adam's apple and a bad case of the hots for Rosie Morales, who, if told Ricky Heimer had died an untimely death, would have replied, "Who?"

When we entered the reception area, Rosie was busy at her word processor, ignoring Ricky, who sat, one hip perched on her desktop. Not that one could blame Ricky. Rosie was an impressive girl. Okay, *woman,* since she just turned nineteen.

She was of medium height and slender, with thick, dark brown hair cascading past her shoulders, a deep olive complexion, black eyes, and a lovely face. She lived at home with her parents while going to Codder Junior College full-time and working for Willis part-time. Her parents paid for her college; Willis paid for her wardrobe—which she proudly showed off every Friday and Saturday night at the Kicker Inn out on the Austin highway. Her ambition, her only waking thought, was to get through junior college and talk her parents into sending her to the University of Houston, where she planned on studying for a career in nutrition and coming back to Codderville for very short visits the rest of her life.

Rosie turned from her word processor when we entered and smiled. "Hey, E.J. Kids." She looked at Bessie and smiled. They'd never met before, but I knew Rosie knew who she was. She reached out and swatted at Ricky. "Get down," she said, not even looking at him.

130

Ricky got down and stood there, hands in pockets, his head bowed, and said, "Hey, Miz Pugh."

"Hi, Ricky. Rosie, is Willis in?"

"Yeah. But he's on the phone with Harry Martin at Wildcatters. We're supposed to find out if we got the bid."

"How's it look?" I asked.

Rosie shrugged, held her hand out straight and wiggled it. *"Comme ci, comme ça."*

"Is that why you're here, Ricky?" I asked.

He nodded, never looking up to make eye contact. I'm not sure I've ever seen Ricky's eyes. They could be blue, green, mauve, chartreuse—who knew?

"Is he in his office or the big room?"

"His office."

I shooed the kids towards the door of the big room. "We'll go in here then and stay out of everybody's way."

"I'll let you know when he's off the phone," Rosie said, fingers already flying across the keyboard again.

Fifteen minutes later Willis came into the big room. His face was long, his eyes downcast. My stomach turned over and died. The Wildcatter's project was the only one Willis had bid on in the last four months. He had some things he was finishing up that would bring in a little cash, but those would soon be over. Without this project it was beans-and-weenies time. And maybe a cardboard box under the nearest bridge.

He looked up at me. "I have bad news," he said.

I sighed, my stomach did the Lambada, the forbidden dance.

Willis said, "I'll have to be out of town at least one week out of every month." His face split into a grin and I whacked him on the shoulder.

"You son of a bitch!"

He whooped and hugged me. "I got it!"

"How much?"

He pulled back. "Jesus, is that all you think about? Money?"

"Yes. How much?"

He grinned. "A hefty commission off a seven-figure bid ain't chicken feed, baby."

I knew Willis didn't want to mention actual figures in front of the kids. But I also knew I'd get the details, since I was the one who balanced the books and bought the groceries. That's the way we did things. Willis made the money and I spent it. It works for us.

"But I will tell you guys one thing," he said to all of us, "it's definitely enough to go out and celebrate."

He walked to the door of the big room and called out to Rosie and Ricky. "You, too. We're going to Carmalita's to celebrate."

Carmalita's was the only classy Mexican restaurant in town. There were some that had better food, but for celebration time, it was Carmalita's. We all piled into Willis' car, with Ricky riding with Rosie in hers, to his delight and her ambivalence. Since Carmalita's was on the highway, on the Black Cat Ridge side of the Colorado, Rosie needed her own transportation to get back to Codderville, where both she and Ricky lived.

Before we left, I'd pulled Willis aside and told him what had happened at the Lesters. "Fuck," he said. "What's going on?"

I shook my head. "I wish I knew. But somebody's obviously looking for something, wouldn't you say?"

"But what?"

I'd shrugged and then the kids had started pulling us towards the door. They never missed an opportunity for Carmalita's.

The restaurant was on the bank of the Colorado with a deck that hung out over the water and tables with large umbrellas scattered over the deck. Since it was barely past four o'clock in the afternoon when we got there, we had the whole place to ourselves. We started with tostadas and hot sauce, a pitcher of margaritas, and Shirley Temples for the kids. It was celebration time. Graham and the girls spent their time pitching pennies at the turtles in the water and trying to feed tostadas to the ducks.

I liked Rosie. I tolerated Ricky. But I couldn't help wishing we were doing what we were supposed to be doing. Celebrating this triumph with Terry and Roy. The way life was meant to be.

# 13

The doorbell started ringing at eight Tuesday morning. I'd had one pitcher of margaritas too many the night before and stumbled out of bed holding my head. Willis snored away on his side of the bed. I grabbed a robe and made it downstairs, cursing the clanging bell that continued to ring. I opened the door to the grim face of my mother-in-law.

"Mrs. Pugh," I said.

She pushed past me. "You two still in bed?" She clicked her tongue against the roof of her mouth, the sound reverberating through my body. Her arms were loaded down with covered dishes. "The rest's out in the car. You gonna go out there like that or are you gonna get some clothes on?"

Without answering, I went upstairs and pulled on some jeans and a sweatshirt, forgoing the amenities, like underwear. Once outside, I opened the back door of her car and looked at the array of foodstuffs sitting on the back seat. So now I knew. She cooked for funerals. For the living she had store-bought donuts and microwave magic. For the dead, she had baked beans, potato salad, fruit Jell-O mold, and an apple pie. I carried the stuff into the dining room, where she'd already laid out the green bean casserole and macaroni salad.

"Some of this stuff needs to be refrigerated. Did you clean out your refrigerator yet?"

Right. Of course. Doesn't everyone right before a funeral? Well, maybe they do, but I'm not all that hep on funerals. I went into the kitchen, grabbed one of the kitchen chairs and the trash can and pulled them both up to the refrigerator. Propping open the door, I sat on the chair and began throwing things indiscriminately into the trash. As Mrs. Pugh brought in her goodies, I shoved them inside. I finally closed the door to the refrigerator, just as the doorbell rang again. I went to it to discover Rosemary Rush standing there with a strawberry three-layer cake in a clear Tupperware cake holder.

"Just thought I'd bring this over before everything gets too hectic," she said, pushing past me and on into my dining room, where she placed the cake holder next to Mrs. Pugh's Tupperware pie holder.

At ten minutes after nine, Doris Maynard, an older lady at the church, brought by a smoked turkey. At nine-thirty, Louanne Bridges brought by chips and dips. At ten-oh-six, Marilou Tanner brought by ten gallons of iced tea and coffee service for one hundred: a huge percolator and cups of saucers. Compliments of the church kitchen. She also had a Mississippi mud pie out on the back seat of her car, if I'd please go get it, the one in the Tupperware pie holder. At ten forty-five, John Edmonds brought by a three bean salad and a chili pie his wife had made. At eleven-fifteen, a woman I didn't know, who said that her name was Candy Mason and that she was the niece of Paula Taylor from the church, brought by chili con queso and three bags of tortilla chips.

By this time, Willis was on his way to the grocery store for ice and two extra Styrofoam ice chests, and Mrs. Pugh was spending her time keeping the kids out of the food on the dining room table.

At twelve noon, when I thought it was over, the door-bell rang again. Willis was upstairs practicing the eulogy he'd finally written himself and figuring out what to wear, Mrs. Pugh was in the living room reading Bible stories to the girls, Graham was in the dining room trying to figure out a way to snitch a piece of pie without anyone noticing, and I was in the kitchen, drinking a cup of coffee and trying to figure out whether killing myself was a valid alternative to existence.

I walked resolutely to the door and opened it. Elena Luna stood on the steps, two large, grease-stained paper bags in her hands, which she shoved in my direction. "From my mother," she said. "Four hundred tamales. All pork." She turned and headed down the steps.

"Luna!" I yelled.

She turned. "What?"

"Want a cup of coffee?"

She walked back up the steps. "Sure," she said, following me into the kitchen.

I poured her a cup and we sat and stared at the coffee machine. She took a sip. "Good coffee."

"Thanks. I grind my own beans."

"No kidding?"

"Yeah. And I use distilled water."

"No shit?"

"Yeah."

"Good coffee."

"Want something to eat?"

She looked around the kitchen at the three Styrofoam

ice chests and at the food on every counter, and we both burst out laughing.

Between bouts of laughter, she said, "I wouldn't want to take food from your kids' mouths."

I gasped and replied, "We're simple folk, we haven't got much, but we share."

The swinging door swung open and Mrs. Pugh stood on the threshold, disapproval emanating from her like gas from a swamp.

Luna and I sobered immediately, like kids in the back pew at church when the usher has pinched their ears.

"It's almost twelve-thirty, E.J. Don't you think you should be getting ready for the service?" Mrs. Pugh said.

I looked at Luna in her black skirt and jacket with her white-bowed blouse. "You're going to the service?" I asked.

She nodded.

"Well," I said, "why don't you stay here and have some more coffee and ride over with Willis and me?"

"Sounds good," she said, lifting her coffee cup and draining the last of it before pouring herself another cup, not once glancing at my mother-in-law. I knew how she felt.

I walked towards the door where Mrs. Pugh still held her ground. "Well," I said, trying to get by her, "I'll just go on upstairs now."

"That's a good idea," she said, folding her arms across her chest and moving slightly so I could get by. I went through the dining room, swatting Graham on the fanny and suggesting he get out of there now, thus asserting myself as a grown-up, something I never felt like when around my mother-in-law.

I pulled out the black dress I'd bought for Willis' father's funeral three years before, the one I'd worn to Rusty's funeral two years before. Maybe I should have burned it. If I'd burned it, maybe Terry would still be alive. God wouldn't make me go to a funeral if I didn't have anything to wear. I shook my head at my own stupidity and pulled the dress on.

Graham had convinced us, despite his grandmother's disapproval, that he should go to the funeral. After what Elaine Comstock, the psychotherapist, had told me, I tended to agree with Graham and shared my views with Willis. Graham was dressed and ready to go when we got downstairs. Mrs. Pugh didn't say anything; of course she never does, but gave us that look when we walked out.

The four of us, Willis, Elena, Graham and I, got to the church around one-thirty. The service was to begin at two, burial at three. We walked to the door of the sanctuary and saw the four caskets lined up at the front, near the lectern. My dancing stomach from the day before returned and I could feel the heat behind my eyes. I could also feel Graham's hand reach out for mine. I held it and squeezed, feeling his grip tighten as his body shuddered. Maybe Mrs. Pugh had been right, I thought. My God, he's only seven. He's such a little shit most of the time that I forget he's just a baby. That a lot of his little-shittiness is just bravado, just testing the boundaries and learning about being a man.

Berry Rush came out of his office on the left of the lobby. "Willis, E.J." He held out both his hands. Like idiots, Willis shook one and I shook the other. He bent toward Graham. "Well, hello, young man. How are you holding up?"

I wanted to smack him. Right in the kisser. I put my hands on Graham's shoulders and squeezed. "He's doing fine," I told Reverend Rush, a grim smile on my face.

Straightening up, he looked at Luna. She held out her hand and he shook it. "Detective Luna, Codderville Police."

"Well," he said, smiling. He turned to Willis. "Why don't we go in my study and discuss your eulogy."

The two men left, leaving Luna and Graham and me standing in the foyer. I walked into the sanctuary and looked around. Despite my notice to the contrary, the sanctuary was filled with flowers. I wondered if the Codderville Children's Foundation had received a dime, other than the little I'd sent myself.

After a few minutes, Willis and Reverend Rush joined us, and we waited silently for two o'clock to arrive. People began arriving at around fifteen till and the sanctuary was filled by two o'clock. I saw no curiosity seekers; just friends. People from the church and the neighborhood who'd known the Lesters for years. And the entire senior class of Codderville High School, which had been let off for the day in honor of Monique, the Student Council Treasurer. There were no strangers with Nikons slithering around the pews. So much for Reverend Rush's theory, I thought to myself. Okay, I gloated to myself.

As there was no family, Willis and I, as executors, and Graham, sat in the front row. We stood for the singing of the hymns and, after Reverend Rush's flawless, lifeless, and gratefully short sermon, he said, "And now, Willis Pugh has a few words for you."

Willis walked up to the lectern and cleared his throat. He put his piece of paper on the podium and looked out at the congregation. "Four years ago, my wife and I, with our little boy and our baby girl, moved from Houston to Black Cat Ridge. We were the second family to move onto the street. The Lesters were the first. I remember the day the movers showed up. They tried to back the van up the driveway but missed and ran onto the Lesters' lawn. Roy came running out of the house. The lawn, at that point, was just sprigs of grass over sandy dirt. He said, 'Hey, fella, your people ran over my grass!" I said I was sorry, but what could I do? He walked across the driveways, into my yard, and yanked up a sprig of my grass. I laughed so hard I thought I'd fall over. We were friends from that moment on."

Willis took a deep breath. I could feel Graham's hand in mine, squeezing until I thought I'd lose the use of my index finger.

"Terry Lester was my wife's best friend. Aldon Lester was my son's best friend. Monique Lester was our baby-sitter and spent hours telling my wife the things she couldn't tell her peers or her mother. Roy Lester was my best friend. I hadn't had a best friend since high school. Grown-up men just don't do that, I suppose. But some-how, Roy and I managed it." His face began to crumble as I held a Kleenex to my own. Willis looked down at the caskets. "We're gonna miss you guys," he said and left the lectern.

Willis resumed his seat next to mine and I put my free arm around his neck and rested my head on his shoulder. Distantly, I heard Reverend Rush dismiss the congregation, telling it where the burial would be and that all were welcome at our house after. The organist played "Amazing Grace" as we exited the sanctuary.

At graveside, sitting in the metal folding chairs under the somber canopy, I glanced around the edges of the cemetery, looking for the killer. In movies and books, there was always somebody lurking next to various tombstones at the burial of murder victims. No one was lurking here. Not even the detective assigned to the case, Doyle Stewart, who should have been.

Like at any good funeral, there wasn't a dry eye in the house as we left the gravesite for the limo and cars parked on the winding drive. We'd found out that the police had notified Roy's aunt at her nursing home in Dallas, but she'd only managed to look up, say "Roy who?" and babble a bit about what they were having for lunch. Terry's mother had been hospitalized for possibly the last time. As the only "family," Willis and I rode with Graham in the limo.

The late afternoon was a bit of a blur, busy as I was serving iced tea and coffee, making sure everyone had something to eat. Every time I passed the dining room, I'd look at the spread on the table and think how much I should want to eat some of it, but my body didn't react in its usual ravenous way. The black dress, a perfect fit when I bought it for my father-in-law's funeral, had been tight for Rusty's. Now, it again fit nicely. As I walked into the kitchen for the millionth time, I thought I should call the *National Enquirer,* let them know I'd discovered a brand-new diet. Just have someone you love murdered. It does wonders for your caloric intake.

For fear of having Bessie overhear conversations centering around her family, we'd asked a girl from the church, Kerrie Smith, a friend of Monique's, to come sit with the girls upstairs while the funeral party raged in the downstairs. Graham held up a wall in the living room, a piece of uneaten cake in one hand, dribbling crumbs on the carpeting. I let it go, figuring the stain it made wouldn't be as bad as the stains on the carpet next door. Everything works out if you just put it in perspective.

The last of the mourners left around nine o'clock. Kerrie came downstairs a little before that, letting us know both girls were sound asleep. Graham moved past her up the stairs, saying good night absently over his shoulder. I would have to think about taking Graham to see Elaine Comstock along with the girls. Maybe we'd all go.

Willis and I stood at the door, shaking hands and hugging, saying those automatic things one says at such an occasion. Berry and Rosemary Rush were the last to leave.

"Now don't you worry about that cake plate," Rosemary said. "I'll be by in the morning to pick it up. Don't even think about washing it." She squeezed my arm and smiled in that Rosemary Rush sort of way. All teeth and cheeks.

Reverend Rush took both my hands in his. "You did beautifully today, E.J. I'm very proud of you. I hope my sermon was to your liking?" He smiled a secret smile, just for the two of us. I nodded my head. He squeezed my hands. "If there's anything I can do. . . . I know you and the children will probably want some counseling before long. I'd be happy to speak with Bessie . . ."

God forbid, I thought. Out loud, I said, "That's been taken care of, Reverend Rush. But thank you so much for the offer. And for all your help." I smiled. All teeth and cheeks. "Good night."

Willis held the door open and they left. Closing it, he looked at me and leaned against it. "You wanna change churches?"

I shook my head. "No. Just preachers."

With our arms around each other's waists, we headed for the kitchen. "Maybe we can start a rumor about Rosemary and their German shepherd," I suggested.

143

# 14

Wednesday morning I drove the kids to school. After a quick call to the counselor, Elaine Comstock, it was determined Bessie should try to go back to the Montessori. Montessori teachers are in a class unto themselves. It's a shame all preschoolers are not allowed such quality, only those whose parents have healthy checking accounts. If some of the money wasn't released soon from the estate, I knew two little girls who would be back at home playing with their Barbies. But that Wednesday morning, the teachers were wonderful. They took Bessie in and explained to the class that Bessie didn't feel like talking right now, but she sure felt like playing. Three little girls were next to her in a flash, all offering the toys in their hands. I left, feeling it might work.

When I got back to my house, Mrs. Pugh sat in the driveway in her 1972 Dodge four-door. She had keys to the house but didn't believe in walking in someone else's home uninvited. There are some good points in her rigid thinking. She got out as I pulled in and began unpacking her back seat. I opened the door of my car and got out, not that my first thought wasn't to flee to the nearest dock and take the slowest boat to anywhere.

"Mrs. Pugh? Hi, what's up?"

She handed me a mop. And a pail. The pail was full of cleansers and tools.

"I figured today was as good a day as any to start on that house," she said, waving abstractly towards the Lesters' home.

"Uh, I was going to call—"

"I know. You were gonna call some service to come out here and do this. Well, there ain't a one in town'll do it. Believe me. 'Sides, I've cleaned up more blood, pee, and crap in my lifetime than you can imagine. There ain't nothing in the human body I haven't scrubbed up one time or another. Let's get to it. There's boxes in the trunk."

I opened the trunk and found flat boxes, rolls of tape, and labels. The woman, if aggravating, was organized. She took the pail and a broom while I struggled with the mop and the boxes. Leaving everything on the back steps, I ran to my house and got the key.

It was surprising what all the vandals hadn't broken. Chairs that were tipped over, when set in an upright position, proved to be in as good a shape as ever. The china in the tipped-over china cabinets was ruined, but the cabinets themselves were fine. Even some of the heavier pieces of china, the teapots and creamer and sugar bowls, were okay. I went to Terry's overflowing newspaper recycle bin, the one thing I hadn't emptied, and brought that into the dining room, where I started wrapping things to save for Bessie: the good silverware, the small silver coffee set they'd gotten as a wedding present, the few salvageable pieces of china. In the bottom bookshelf in the living room, I found the picture

146

albums. Ten of them, full of wedding pictures, Monique as a baby, Aldon as a baby, and Bessie as a baby. They'd been rifled, but not destroyed. A couple of paintings were okay, some pillows, a few of Bessie's videotapes, some knickknacks, books, end tables, the dining room table, the Tupperware in the kitchen, some pots and pans.

Upstairs, some of the clothing had been trampled but not ripped, some of the bedding was okay. Cufflinks and tie clasps were scattered across the dressing table but were okay. None of it was expensive, but they were things that belonged to Bessie's father. I kept them. Along with some of Terry's costume jewelry and Monique's gold two-heart necklace given to her by a boyfriend the year before. One of Aldon's model planes was still intact, some of his books, one of his Nintendo tapes. The fish from his aquarium lay shriveled and dead on the floor from the hole in the side of the glass. A quicker death, really, than the one I'd been giving them, having forgotten their existence and their need for food.

In a separate box, one to be taken to my house, I put the salvageable things from Bessie's room: a few clothes, some dolls, her curtains that matched the comforter I'd already taken to our house. I worked on automatic pilot, going from room to room sporadically, gleaning what I could from the mess that abounded. Mrs. Pugh, meanwhile, scrubbed walls and carpeting and doors, trying to take away the mess and gore left behind after four murders. It's not an easy thing to do. That memory wanted to stay, and stay it did, in rusty brown stains on light beige carpet, in rusty brown streaks on oyster white walls and doors.

"We're gonna haveta rip up this carpet," Mrs. Pugh pronounced. "And paint." She shook her head. "We waited too long. Shoulda been cleaned the same night."

Right, I thought. Excuse me, Mr. Policeman, Mr. Coroner, but I need to scrub up here if you've gotten those nasty old bodies out.

"As soon as they release some of the money from the estate, I'll get it done," I said.

"Well, you done with all the stuff?"

"Yes, ma'am."

She nodded her head. "Okay then." Mrs. Pugh looked at me and patted me on the arm. "It ain't ever easy, E.J." She left through the back door then, pulling her pail and broom behind her.

I watched my mother-in-law as she loaded her car and drove off, wondering if it was she who was changing or if it was me. Was she being nice, or was I just noticing it for the first time? The thought occurred to me that this woman, who'd lost two of the three most important people in her life (her husband and one of her two sons), could finally relate to me in my loss and grief. I knew part, the biggest part, of my own dislike for her had been because I knew she never approved of me, never liked me, didn't accept me as part of the family. But after twelve years of her disapproval, could I change now? Could I accept her? Or had all this "niceness" just been something I'd dreamed up? Did she still dislike me as much as ever?

Shaking my head, I grabbed some boxes, putting ones for storage in the back of the station wagon. I went in my house and called the two "you-store-it" places in town, finding a small space for a nominal amount. I'd get Willis to help me with the furniture. I was going to save everything salvageable. It wasn't my decision on what to save and what not to save. It was Bessie's. And it could wait until she was well enough and old enough to make that decision. I drove my salvage boxes to the storage space, signed yet another contract, and placed the boxes in the corners, out of the way, leaving room for the furniture.

On the drive back to my house, I got to thinking. Was

148

this what I was going to do? Let the little details of the living brush away the memories of the dead? Had the funeral signified the end of not only the Lester family but also my curiosity about who had killed them? No, it was still there, nagging in the back of my mind. But Luna said leave it alone. Ed Jones was working on it from the Commission angle. He'd have something soon. It was the business of the police, not some housewife–cum–romance writer. Who the hell did I think I was? Nancy Drew?

But on the other hand, who knew the Lesters better? I was a college-educated, fairly intelligent and intuitive woman. Okay, so I hadn't been acting like it, running around giving stupid interviews to the paper. But I was still in grief then. Now I was thinking better. The memory of the Lester family shouldn't be one of doubt and suspicion. Not to mention there were insurance policies that wouldn't pay off until it was proved Roy didn't commit the murders and suicide. Not his office policy, but others. And Bessie deserved that money. It was hers. It was her education, her wedding, her first house, her first baby. Her future.

I turned the car around and headed back to Codderville. I was going to talk with Detective Elena Luna. And she wasn't going to like what I had to say one little bit.

She sat at her desk, talking on the phone. I sat down in the chair next to her, my purse in my lap, my hands clasped on top of it as primly as my mother-in-law would have done. She turned away from me, continuing her discussion on the phone, trying in vain to ignore my existence. I sat. I wasn't budging. Finally, the conversation over, Detective Luna had nothing left to do but put the receiver back in the hook and turn to me. Which she did.

"What?" she said, her voice as gracious as if she were

149

on the receiving end of fourteen Seventh-Day Adventists on her front porch.

"So, what's Ed Jones got to say these days?"

She turned to her desktop, picking up a random sheet of paper. Without looking at me, she said, "Drop it, E.J."

I shook my head. Noticing she hadn't noticed, I leaned in closely, usurping her spacing, and shook my head again. "Uh-uh," I said. "I'm not dropping it. Roy doesn't deserve that and neither does Bessie."

Luna sighed, picked up the phone, and dialed. "Ed Jones," she said after a minute's pause. "Detective Elena Luna, Codderville P.D."

I sat. She sat. Finally, she said, "Mr. Jones. Hi, sorry to bother you. About the Lester business . . . uh-huh . . . yes . . . well . . . the thing is . . . uh-huh . . . Mr. Jones . . . uh-huh . . . the reason I'm calling . . . uh-huh . . . I'm sending someone to your office." She hung up the phone. She scribbled an address down on a slip of paper and handed it to me. "You deal with the pontificating bastard," she said, turning back to her paperwork.

The county attorney's office was in the same building as the police department: the county courthouse. Except it was in the main part of the building, on the third floor. I rode up in the ornate elevator with possibly the last living elevator operator as company. I had no idea the county attorney was so inaccessible, but I had to go through three women and a man to get to him, telling each the police had just called and sent me up. Ed Jones' office rivaled that of the president of the school board, who had the most gorgeous office I'd seen to date (we won't discuss the conditions of the schools or the food served to the children while he sat in multithousand-dollar splendor).

The walls were heavily paneled in real oak, the desk topped with marble. The leather chairs and couches were shiny with wax and the frames on the paintings on the walls were gilt. His suit cost more than most of Willis's wardrobe and his shoes shone like the couches. Neither the expensive suit nor the shoes hid the fact that Ed Jones was a short, slight, gnomelike, completely bald man with glasses and a protruding upper lip.

He didn't stand when I entered, but being a feminist, that didn't bother me, even though I knew he intended for it to. Looking up, but just barely, he said, "And you are?"

"E. J. Pugh, coexecutor of the estate of Roy and Terry Lester."

He pointed at one of the leather chairs. "Sit," he said. I sat. "Why do you want to see me?"

"I understand you're investigating the . . . trouble at the Utility Commission. I also understand there might be some connection to Roy Lester. As guardian to the Lesters' only living child, I'm concerned that Roy's reputation be unsullied as soon as possible." I can be, when pushed, as Berry Rushesque as the next guy.

"What sort of connection do you understand there to be, Mrs. Pugh? Other than the fact that Roy Lester was the manager of the Utility and ultimately responsible for any . . . shenanigans going on at the Utility."

" 'Shenanigans'? Misappropriation of funds you call 'shenanigans'?" I asked, raising my eyebrows to show my surprise at his choice of word. I would have raised one to show my skepticism, but I can't physically do that. More's the pity.

"No charges have been filed."

"When will charges be filed?" I asked, the eyebrows still in position.

"Against whom?" he asked, his bushy brows mimicking mine.

"Against anyone!" Luna had been right. He was a pontificating bastard.

"I am not at liberty to discuss that at this time," he

replied, his eyebrows and his head both going down, his head toward his papers, as if I'd already been dismissed.

I sighed. "Mr. Jones. I'm not the press. I'm an interested party. I hope you can see that as guardian of Elizabeth Lester, it's my responsibility—"

His head jerked up and his body became rigid. "You may not *be* the press, Mrs. Pugh, but you certainly seem to be indiscriminate in your dealings with them."

Jesus. Was I ever going to live down blabbing to Armstead Pucker?

"My lips are sealed, Mr. Jones. I've learned my lesson the hard way dealing with the press. Now, as I was saying, it's my responsibility—"

"To feed and clothe Elizabeth Lester. To bind her wounds and heal her spirit. It is not your responsibility to go blindly charging into matters that do not concern you. Let me be perfectly frank—"

"Please. Don't pull any punches with me, Ed," I said.

"To be perfectly frank, Mrs. Pugh," he said, ignoring my comment, "you have no business in my office, much less demanding information concerning an ongoing investigation." He stood. "Now, if you'll excuse me, I have work to do." He walked to the door and held it for me. I was getting goddamned tired of people ushering me out of places. Really, *really* tired.

I'd been holding in my rage over what had happened to my friends for over a week. I'd been ignored by the police, talked down to by my preacher, and tolerated by my husband. But I'd be damned if I'd let some two-bit lawyer in a fancy suit shove me around. Okay, so I was venting. A woman has a right to vent. Especially to a pontificating bastard like Ed Jones.

I grabbed the door from his hand and slammed it shut. With my five feet eleven inches towering over his five feet three inches, I pressed him against the wall of his office, using only my anger. I swear, I didn't lay a hand on the man. With my finger only inches from his piglike nose, I said, "I just buried four people! Two of them children! Right now I have a little four-year-old girl in my care who was traumatized so badly she can't speak! Anything—*anything*—that has to do with Roy Lester is my business, buster, and don't you forget it! If you have *any* evidence that could show that one of the Utility directors had anything to do with what happened, I want to know it and I want to know it now! Do you understand me?"

"Mrs. Pugh, I could have you arrested!"

I held my hands up. "For what? I haven't touched you! But you have me arrested, I'll come back and use that chrome dome of yours like a bowling ball! Now, one more time, what evidence do you have?"

He shook his head. "I don't have anything that will stand up in court . . ."

"I could give a great big shit about court! What have you got?"

He shrugged and whined, "Rumors. That's all. Nothing more than rumors!"

I stuck my chest out, blocking his vision with a boob. "Tell me!"

"Simon Davidson's ex-secretary said he flew to New Orleans for Mardi Gras and put it down on Utility expense sheets."

"And?" I demanded.

He looked down at the floor. "That's all."

*"What?"* I was momentarily speechless; could do nothing but stare into the ugly face of Ed Jones. Finally, pressing further into his space, I said, "That's what all this brouhaha in the papers has been about? Somebody fudged on their fucking expense account?"

"Move away from me, Mrs. Pugh! I mean it!" I moved. He ran around me toward his desk. "I'm calling the police!" he yelled, picking up the phone. "You won't make it out of this building! I'll have you arrested and your ass in jail, you bitch! I'll throw the book at you! You won't see daylight for years! Assaulting an officer of the court!''

I turned back and smiled. He stood still, looking at me, the telephone receiver in one hand. ''I never touched you,'' I said sweetly. ''Besides, can't you just see the headline? 'County attorney Edward Jones was physically abused today by housewife Eloise Pugh. Mrs. Pugh, unarmed, held Attorney Jones hostage for ten minutes by sheer might.'' I grinned. That's one good thing about male chauvinism. It can be used.

County Attorney Edward Jones put the telephone receiver down. ''Don't get a ticket in this town, Mrs. Pugh. Don't put out too much garbage or forget to bring your garbage cans in. Hope your son never skateboards on a sidewalk or your daughter jaywalks. Hope your husband never wants a city contract, Mrs. Pugh. Because I can make life very difficult for you.''

Again, I grinned. ''If any of those things happen, Mr. Jones, I'll just be waiting for you some night in your garage.''

I left. So maybe it wasn't the smartest move of my life. But who's to know? I didn't think Ed Jones would brag about his afternoon with anyone. And I certainly wasn't telling.

Okay. So Simon Davidson, chairman of the board of directors of the Codder County Utility, had fudged on his expense account. In this age of S&L scandals, I doubt if anyone other than Ed Jones could get too excited about that. No one, not Davidson, no one, could get excited enough about it to kill four people. If Ed Jones was telling the truth, and I for one think he was, then there could be no connection between the murders of the Lester family and the ''shenanigans'' at the Utility.

I was back to square one. Maybe it was about time I did what I told Armstead Pucker I was going to do. Call in a private eye. But where in the hell did you find a private eye in rural Texas? And then I remembered, when Marilou Tanner's little boy had been molested the year before, the Tanners had hired an investigator because the police said they didn't have enough evidence to go against the sixty-five-year-old retired mailman neighbor whom their son had accused. The PI had found the evidence, and also found three other little boys in the neighborhood who'd been molested by the same guy.

I pulled up to the next pay phone, jumped out, and dialed Marilou's number.

"Hey, it's E.J."

Marilou laughed. "Thank God for call waiting! I've been on the phone for over half an hour with Rosemary Rush. Just let me tell her I have to get off."

"No wait, Marilou, you can still use the excuse, but first I need the number of that investigator ya'll used last year."

"E.J. You're really going to do it?"

"You bet your ass I'm gonna do it."

"Well, his name's Malcolm Dobbins and he's really good. He's in La Grange. Hold on. Let me get rid of La Dame Rush and I'll get you the number."

I waited on hold for a couple of minutes. Then, "Okay. Here it is. Malcolm Dobbins. *D-O-B-B-I-N-S*." She read me the number in La Grange. "Good luck, hon."

I said, "Thanks," and hung up. I decided to get back in my car and go home to call La Grange. A real-life private eye. Rural Texas variety. Should prove interesting.

# 15

I dialed the number of Malcolm Dobbins in La Grange. A recording said, "Hi, this is Dobbins Investigation. We'll be out of the office until May first. Please call back then or leave a message. Thank you."

Great. It was now the second week in April and this jerk wouldn't be back in town until the first of May. Okay, I'd call back. If I hadn't solved the whole thing myself before then. Right. Nancy's the name. Detection's the game.

Checking the time, I headed out to pick up the kids. The guilt started upon seeing the girls. How could I, a mother, have behaved the way I had with Ed Jones? Okay, so I was venting. What kind of excuse is venting? I had a few pent-up emotions and I spilled them all over Ed Jones. Why? Because he was smaller than me? That made me no better than men who battered women. Taking out my anger on the first weaker victim I could find. Jones was right. He should have had me arrested. Thrown away the key.

I got out of the car and hugged the girls. Equally. "How'd it go?" I asked their general vicinity.

"We played," Megan said. Bessie nodded agreement.

"You have a good time?" I asked.

"Oh, yeah. We learned about birthing babies," Megan said. Bessie nodded agreement.

Birthing babies? Four-year-olds? "What kind of babies?" I asked. One learns to ask these questions, generally, before one goes screaming to the school board.

"Tater poles," Megan said. Bessie nodded agreement.

" 'Tater poles'?" Potatoes having babies? A little botany lesson?

"Baby frogs. Tater poles," Megan said, exasperated at her mother's obvious stupidity.

"Oh! *Tadpoles.*"

"That's what I said. Tadpoles." Megan shook her head and crawled in on the back seat. I looked to the door of the school and saw the girls' teacher coming out.

"You two buckle up and I'll be right here talking with Miss Rita."

With one eye on the car, I walked over to Miss Rita. "How'd she do?" I asked.

She sighed. "Great, I guess. She played as long as it wasn't a touching game."

"Pardon?"

"Any game where the children touched, ring-around-the-rosy, London-bridge, anything like that, she wouldn't do it. She'd sit down and watch. She didn't cry or act out or anything. She'd just sit down and watch."

No touching games. Yet she let me hug her. And Ruby Gale, her old nursery teacher at church. But, come to think of it, I don't remember her and my kids touching, hugging, hitting, anything like that. Info to file away for Elaine.

"Do you think I should bring her back tomorrow?" I asked Miss Rita.

"Definitely. Unless your counselor tells you otherwise. She seemed to have a good time and she participated in everything. Except, like I said, the touching games."

I nodded and thanked her and got back in the car. We went on to the elementary school to pick up Graham.

You know, guilt's a funny thing. Instead of going home, I finally did something I'd been thinking about doing since I'd seen Bessie playing with my mother-in-law's cocker, Winston. I took the kids to the animal shelter. Graham went straight for a Doberman and pit bull mix. I told him no firmly and ushered him over to the kitten section.

"I don't want a stupid kitten!" he said.

"Okay. Fine. Don't get one. Each of the girls is going to get a kitten though."

Megan yelled, "Yay!" and ran for the pens, a wide-eyed Bessie right behind her.

"I want a dog!" Graham said, leaning against the fence, his arms crossed over his bony chest and his lower lip doing its diving board imitation.

"Sorry, kiddo. No dogs at the moment. A kitten. You can name it anything you want."

"Yeah?"

"Yeah."

Grudgingly, he pushed himself away from the fence and walked to the pens where the kittens were. Megan had already picked up and discarded almost every kitten there without deciding. Bessie, on the other hand, sat on the ground, a small, yellow tabby cat in her arms, her Ernie doll discarded beside her. I knelt down next to her.

"Is that the one you want?" I asked.

She nodded her head vigorously.

I smiled. "Okay then, it's yours. May I see it?"

She handed me the kitten and I held up its tail. "Hum. I think it's a boy. Is that okay?"

She nodded her head and I handed the kitten back.

"What do you want to name him?"

She sat there stroking his soft fur for a minute, then looked at me, giving me her first real smile. She pointed at her Ernie doll.

"Ernie?" I asked. "You want to name him Ernie?"

Bessie nodded her head.

Megan came running around the pen, holding a black kitten with white boots and a white face. "Then this one's Bert!" she said. She and Bessie grinned at each other.

Graham came up with a stubby, mottled kitten with a chewed-up left ear. "Meet Axl Rose," he said, grinning from ear to ear.

I wrote a check for the kittens and put all three kids in the cargo area of the station wagon with their charges. I know it's not safe, but I figured it was safer than having three kittens running around under my feet while I drove. If Ed Jones saw, I figured I'd be under the jailhouse for that one.

I parked in front of the grocery store, leaving the kids in the care of Graham (okay, another unmotherly thing to feel guilty about) and ran in for supplies: cat food, kitty litter, flea collars, a catnip mouse and three balls with bells, and a rattan basket with a fluffy pillow, big enough for all three kittens. Once at home, we set up the utility room as the cathouse and put bowls of milk on the floor in the kitchen. Graham tired of Axl Rose in about ten minutes. With Megan it took all of fifteen. Bessie stayed there the rest of the afternoon, lying on the floor watching Ernie or holding him in her arms.

Around six that evening, dinner percolating in my mind, Willis called.

"I don't know when I'll be home."

"Hello to you too, dear," I said.

"Sorry."

"What's going on?"

He sighed. "This new fucking project."

160

"Oh. So now it's a 'fucking' project. Last week it was the greatest thing since sliced bread."

"Perspective, my dear, perspective. Last week the project wasn't mine."

"Makes sense to me. When do you think you'll be home?"

"August."

"I love it when you're reasonable," I said.

"I don't know, babe. Late. I'll have a pizza sent in for Ricky and me."

"Is Rosie staying late?"

"Jealous?"

I laughed. "Just thinking about perks for Ricky."

"Naw. He's gonna have to wing it without her. It will be a challenge for him, but I think he's man enough."

"You know, if you got off the phone and started working, idiot, maybe you'd be home at a decent hour."

"What? And no overtime?"

I snorted. "Overtime. What a concept."

"I'll call you later," Willis said. "Kiss the kids for me. Love you."

"Love you, too."

I put the chicken I had defrosting on the countertop into the meat keeper in the refrigerator and called the pizza place. I wouldn't have thought of it if a certain person hadn't mentioned it. I made a quick salad and had it on the table by the time the delivery boy showed up.

Bessie wanted to eat with her kitten on her lap. I had to make a quick decision. Tell her no now, with a possible reprimand if necessary, or learn to regret it later. I told her no. She looked at me with those big, cocker spaniel brown eyes and gently placed Ernie on the kitchen floor. I didn't pick him right back up and place him in her lap. I was proud of myself for that.

I watched TV with the kids until eight-thirty, then supervised baths and got them to bed by nine-thirty. There was nothing on the boob tube, so I closed up the house, turning off lights, and started to go to bed. At the bottom of the stairs, I stopped. I wasn't tired. I turned and went to my office under the stairs and turned on the computer, closing the door behind me so the noise, if I decided to print, wouldn't disturb the kids. I hadn't worked in so long I couldn't remember what had been happening to Lady Leslie and her hunk. I skipped back two chapters and began to read to get into the flow of it, such as it was. At 10:03 by my digital clock, the electricity went off.

I sat stock still in the pitch black of my office. There was no storm. Why had the lights gone off? Okay, it happens, I told myself. Somebody tripped a wire at the main switch place. Or something. I got up and opened the door to the office. The kitchen was only a few steps away to the right. In the kitchen were flashlights and candles and matches. There was no moon that night and the street light was at the end of the block, on the other side of the people next door to the Lesters' house. Its weak illumination did little to lighten my dark kitchen in the back of the house. I closed my eyes and held on to the wall, willing myself to get used to the darkness. When I opened my eyes I could see much better. Strangely enough, I could hear better, too. And what I could hear ran a shiver down my spine and turned the contents of my stomach to sulfuric acid.

I heard the window in the dining room opening. It makes a slight screech sound when it opens, the sound of aluminum scraping aluminum. I heard a voice whisper, ''Shit, man, you'll wake 'em up.''

I heard another voice whisper hoarsely, ''Fuck you.''

I heard the thump of a foot on the carpeted floor, then another, and another, and another.

They were in my house. ''They,'' the ones who'd killed my friends, the ones who'd tried to run me off the road, the ones who'd vandalized the house next door, the ones

162

who were going to kill me and my kids. And I stood frozen in the little hall between the kitchen and the utility room, unable to move my eyelids, much less my body.

"You take care of the ones upstairs while I check out down here," one whispered.

Upstairs, I thought. Oh, my God. Upstairs. The kids. I moved, quietly, stealthily, into the kitchen. I was almost to the counter when I hit the bowl of milk on the floor for the kittens. It skittered across the room, making a noise not unlike a cherry bomb in the toilet.

I whirled towards the opening from the kitchen into the dining room. A male form was standing there, his hand pointing at me. I fell to the floor as the bright flash of his gun blinded me and the muffled "thump" of the report reverberated like thunder in the quiet house. I rolled toward the opening and kicked up as high and as hard as I could with my leg. By his guttural response and his bent-over position, I knew I'd connected with the groin, as I'd been hoping for.

I scrambled to my feet and ran toward the counter where I kept my knives. He grabbed my hair, pulling me backwards. I twisted in his grasp, seeing the dim glint of the gun in his hand. With both hands clasped together, I hit his arm with all my might, sending the gun flying behind us, into the dining room.

"You fucking bitch," he spat, no longer whispering, his grasp on my hair tightening and twisting. Then, for a moment, I was free, his hand off my hair. Before I could react, it was around my throat. I now knew his choice of my demise. I would be strangled to death.

This was my kitchen. I had the advantage of knowing the territory. I reached behind me for the butcher block slab that held my knives. I grabbed the handle of the largest knife and pulled. Instead of the knife coming out and stabbing my assailant, the entire butcher block slab came with my hand, slamming against the side of his

163

head. Stunned, his grasp on my throat lessened, but not enough. I hit him again. And again.

Finally, he fell to his knees, his hands up to protect his bleeding head.

How many nights have I spent in front of the TV, watching the heroine in some dumb made-for-TV movie hit the bad guy and run? How many times have I heard my husband grunt and say, "Jesus, finish him off, stupid." Enough.

I hit him again and again, until his whole body fell to the floor. And then I hit him again. And again. Until the butcher block slab split in two in my hands, the matching hickory knives falling on the body on my kitchen floor. I stood up and looked down at the man. His face was so messed up I doubt if I'd have recognized him if I knew him. I kicked him, mostly to see if he was conscious. He wasn't. I wondered if I'd killed him. But only for a moment. There was someone else upstairs with my kids. I grabbed the flashlight out of the drawer and raced for the dining room where the gun had flown earlier. I picked it up and flashed the light on it.

My father had shown me a gun when I was a teenager. He'd bought it because two houses in the neighborhood had been burglarized. He showed me the safety and how to remove it. He showed me how to hold it and how to fire. Two days later, Mother made him sell it. But I remembered. Thank you, Daddy, I thought.

I put one of the smaller knives in the back pocket of my bluejeans and held the gun in both hands, the flashlight under my left arm, and headed for the front of the house and the stairs. I froze as the front door slowly began to open.

# 16

Willis stuck his head around the door. "Eej?" he called softly.

I grabbed his arm and pulled him inside, slamming a hand over his mouth. "They're here!" I whispered. "One's upstairs and one's in the kitchen."

He looked wide-eyed towards the kitchen. I shook my head. "It's okay. I think I killed him." I caught a giggle coming halfway out of me. I hoped to hell it was just nerves. The only other alternative was I was a secret homicidal maniac.

He removed my hand. "Baby, you okay?"

I nodded. He looked down at the gun in my hand. "Where the fuck'd that come from?"

I nodded toward the kitchen. "Willis, one's upstairs with the kids."

Slowly, he looked toward the top of the stairs. "Jesus," he breathed. He took the gun from my hand. "Does the phone work?"

I ran as quietly as possible into the living room and picked up the receiver. Dead as the proverbial doornail. Whatever the hell that is. I ran back to Willis and shook my head.

With his mouth close to my hear, he said, "Go next door and call Luna."

I shook my head. "I'm not leaving you."

"Fuck that. Do it!" His voice was soft but his grip on my arm wasn't.

I moved quickly into the kitchen, skirting around the body on the floor, and grabbed the Lesters' housekey off the ring inside the Tupperware cabinet. Skirting the body once again, I made it to the back door, gingerly flipped back the deadbolt lock, and slid out into the darkness of the back yard.

I made a dash for the Lesters' back door, the key hitting everywhere but the keyhole as I fumbled in the dark. Finally it went in and I turned the key. The blow in the back shoved me through the door and onto the tiles. I heard the door slam as I looked back. A man's outline stood in silhouette against the lightly curtained window of the door. Was this the man who'd been with my kids, or was this a third member of the group?

"You're a hard bitch to kill," he said.

I sat up and scooted backwards, quickly blocked by the legs of the kitchen table.

He laughed. It wasn't a particularly friendly laugh. "No place to run, baby, no place to hide. Come to daddy," he cooed.

He'd taken his first step towards me when the door behind him crashed forward off its hinges, landing on the man with the gun. The gun skittered across the floor, but the bad guy wasn't going for it. He was under the door and Willis' two hundred and something pounds were standing on top of him.

166

Jumping to my feet, I asked Willis, "Are the kids okay?"

He nodded. "Sound asleep."

"You sure they're asleep? Not . . ."

He nodded. "I used Graham's flashlight. They're okay."

Willis leaned over from his stance on the broken door and switched on the kitchen light. I went for the gun where it lay on the floor, next to the refrigerator. I handed it to Willis, who got off the door. I flipped the broken wood and glass off our prisoner. "Call the cops," Willis told me.

I ran to the wall phone and dialed Luna's number at home. A sleepy voice answered "Luna."

"Hey, it's E.J."

"Jesus. A body could get tired of you."

"Two guys broke into my home tonight. I think I killed one of them. The other one we have. He was after our kids. Would you like to do something about this?"

"Where are you now?"

"At the Lesters' house."

"What in the hell are you . . . never mind. Who's with the kids?"

My heart began to race. "Nobody."

"Get over there."

I didn't hear anything else she had to say. I took the butcher knife out of my back pocket where I'd put it what seemed hours before and I ran in the unlocked back door of my home, the flashlight still in my hand, and ran up the stairs. The kids were still asleep. No one was in the house. Unless they were hiding in the attic crawl space. I checked. They weren't.

Going to the back door again, I met Willis and Mr. X coming in. Willis flipped on the kitchen light. "They'd turned off the main switch at the breaker."

I didn't look behind me at the mess I'd made on the floor. Instead I said, "Should I get the kids up?"

Willis thought a moment. "No. . . . Just check 'em again."

I nodded and went back upstairs, turning on the overhead lights this time to make sure. They still slept, without bloodstains or bullet wounds.

By the time I got back downstairs, I could hear the sirens turning onto our street. I went to the front door and opened it. Luna's private car, an antique Chevy Malibu, pulled in first, followed by two patrol cars and an ambulance. Well, I thought, I finally got somebody's attention. That's when I sat down on the first step of the stairs and started bawling. And that's how Luna found me, crying my eyes out, holding a butcher knife in one hand and a flashlight in the other.

She knelt down in front of me. "The kids . . . ," she started.

I nodded. "They're okay," I got out. I pointed towards the kitchen. "They're in there. The dead one. And the live one. With Willis."

She left me, leading her troops towards the kitchen. I sat on the step for only a few minutes when it dawned on me the live one might tell Luna something. Something important. I asked myself if I could stand being in the same room with the body I'd created. I answered myself that I could.

I went into the kitchen. Luna was supervising the cuffing of the live one, the one who had tried to kill me. I got my first look at him in the light. Smugly, I thought I could have taken him. If he hadn't had a gun, of course. He was a scrawny guy in his late twenties, with a weaselly-looking face. A face I'd never seen before.

The paramedics knelt by the other. Who moaned. I leaned up against the wall and felt my body relax. I hadn't killed him. Thank you, God, I prayed. I hadn't

168

killed the son of a bitch. Gingerly, I took a peek over the counter at the mess I'd created on my sparkling clean tile. I was right. I wouldn't be able to recognize this one if I knew him. I suppressed an urge to gag and leaned back against the wall. At least he was alive. There was that.

Roughly, Luna pushed the live one (well, the other live one, the first live one—anyway, you know which one I mean) into one of our kitchen chairs.

"What's your name?" she asked.

He spat at her. Lovely. It landed on my clean kitchen floor. Well, it was clean, other than the blood and stuff over by the counters.

The heel of Luna's boot came down hard on the guy's instep. He let out a cry. "Oh, I'm sorry," Luna said, smiling. "I need to watch where I'm walking."

"Bitch," he muttered.

"What's your name?"

One of the uniforms handed Luna a wallet he'd taken from the guy when he'd frisked him. Luna opened it. "Larry Douglas." She smiled. "Well, Larry. Looks like you two picked the wrong family to mess with this time."

"Fuck you, bitch," Larry said.

"Who paid you to do this, Larry?" He looked at the floor. "Or you just do it for kicks, huh, man?"

"Fuck you, bitch," Larry said.

Luna sighed. "Now that's pathetic, Larry. Repeating your comebacks that way. Really pitiful."

She nodded to one of the uniforms. "Get this scum behind bars, Billy, okay? I don't want him stinking up this lovely home."

The paramedics were loading the other one onto a stretcher. One of the uniforms handed Luna the second wallet. She opened it. "Clyde Hayden. How's old Clyde doing, doc?" she asked the paramedic.

He shook his head. "He'll probably live, but I doubt his

own mother's gonna wanna kiss him when this mess heals."

Luna looked at the messed-up face, then back at me. "Remind me never to get you really riled, okay, Pugh?"

I looked down at the floor, tears beginning to escape again. Willis came up and put his arms around me and I buried my face in his shirt.

"When you two get through with the mushy stuff, you wanna come sit over here and tell me what the hell happened?" Luna asked.

We sat and I told her my part of the story. When I got to the front door opening, Willis took up the tale. "I came home and noticed all the lights in the house were out. We always leave a light or two burning. It made me nervous. Anyway, E.J. told me what had happened and I sent her to the Lesters' to call you, and I went upstairs. I heard one of the kids' windows opening and saw the guy jump off the roof. I ran downstairs and outside and was going to tell E.J. the coast was clear when I heard him inside the Lesters' house with her." He stopped for a minute, looking down at the tabletop. "I guess I just sorta went nuts."

Luna looked at me. I smiled and touched the back of my hand to Willis' cheek. "He broke the door down. Just like the Incredible Hulk."

Willis looked at me looking at him and smiled. When Luna left, she said to me, in an aside, "Should be some great sex going on around here tonight," and left.

She was right. Even the presence of uniformed cops (one outside and one reading in the living room) didn't stop the lust inspired by the adrenaline rush of our experiences that night. It was like the first time: a little wild, very crazy, with clothes half on and half off. But better. Because this time, after twelve years of wedded bliss, we knew each other's buttons.

The next day, Willis called Rosie and told her to have Ricky continue working on whatever they'd been working on the night before. That he'd call but wouldn't be in that day. We kept the kids out of school, afraid now to even try for normalcy. Instead, we all headed for the police station.

The uniform who'd sat with the kids on the day of the discovery at the Lester house, Becks, got called into service again, while Willis and I met with Detective Stewart, Detective Luna, and Police Chief Catfish Watkins.

"Well, Miz Pugh, you got you one healthy right jab on you, lady," Chief Watkins said, laughing.

I didn't find the situation that amusing but decided not to try to show the asshole the politically correct response to such an occurrence. Instead, I smiled wanly, yet bravely I thought, and said, "It worked out, I guess."

"Well, I think we got us a bit of a problem, here. I unnerstand from Detective Luna you been calling her a lot about this stuff with Roy Lester's family."

"Off and on. Whenever anything's occurred that I thought might warrant police involvement." Nicely put, I thought.

"Well, now, Miz Pugh, this here case rightly belongs to Detective Stewart, you know?"

I nodded. "I understand that, Chief. But Detective Stewart has been unwilling to help me."

"That's a goddamn lie!" Stewart yelled, raising himself out of his chair.

Chief Watkins motioned for him to sit. "Now, Doyle, don't get your bowels in an uproar." To me, he said, "What makes you say that, Miz Pugh?"

"From the beginning I've been trying to convince someone, anyone, that Roy Lester did not murder his family and then commit suicide. Detective Stewart seemed unresponsive to that suggestion. Detective Luna told me on many different occasions that the case belonged to Detective Stewart but she seemed the more receptive to my theories. So I continued to call her."

171

Catfish Watkins leaned back in his swivel chair, his elbows on the arms of it, steepling his fingers in front of his face. He smiled. ''So it's what you might call a woman thing?'' he said.

''Pardon?'' I looked from him to Luna, who was looking at the floor.

''You felt you could have a better . . . what d'ya call it, *rapport* with Detective Luna because she's a woman?''

I shrugged. ''Well, yes, I guess that's partly true . . .''

He sat up abruptly and looked at Stewart. ''See there, Doyle, told you it was something like that, didn't I?'' Chief Watkins stood up and ushered us all to his door. ''Now, I sure am glad we got this all cleared up. And Elena, you keep on helpin' out Miz Pugh here, alrighty? Doyle, this is still your case, of course, but Elena here's gonna help you out. Now ain't that right, Elena, honey?''

Luna smiled. A stiff, mouth-only smile, but a smile. ''Certainly, Chief.''

''See there, Doyle?'' he said, slapping Detective Stewart on the back as he closed the glass door to his office.

We stood in the corridor, Luna, Stewart, Willis, and I. Four people who'd just been run up a flagpole and saluted, put in a pipe and smoked, etc., etc. In other words, been given the runaround to beat all runarounds. I smiled to myself. Catfish Watkins was as good a politician as I'd ever seen in action.

''Well,'' Luna finally said, looking at Stewart.

''You interrogate the suspect yet?'' he asked, glaring at her.

''No. I just got in. Had a rough night.''

''Well. Go do it. Let me know what he says.'' And with that, Stewart was gone. To breakfast, we supposed.

If looks could kill, Stewart's back would have been full of buckshot from the glares he was receiving from Elena Luna.

''Ya'll wanna watch this?'' she asked.

Willis and I nodded, and she led us to a little room separated from the interrogation room by a one-way mirror. We had the glass side of the mirror and a speaker attached to a microphone inside the interrogation room. A stenographer sat in one corner of the interrogation room, a large, uniformed policeman stood by the door, and Larry Douglas sat at a table smoking. A plainclothes detective came into the room with Willis and me and we all sat silently watching as Luna entered the interrogation room and started her interview.

"Well, hey, Larry, how you doing?"

Douglas snorted smoke but didn't say anything.

Luna had a piece of paper in her hand. Brandishing it, she said, "Got a little information on you, Larry. Interesting reading. Know what it says?"

Douglas didn't answer.

"Course this sheet only tells me what you been up to as an adult, but we can dig up your juvie records if we need 'em. But, let's see: 1985, assault with a deadly weapon, two to five at Huntsville, out in two and a half; 1987, rape, charges dropped; 1987, another rape, this time the lady stuck with it. Ten to twenty at Huntsville. Oh, what's this? Appealed and won a new trial and this time the lady didn't testify? Convenient for you, honey, really. So, what? You did a year, year and half on that one?"

Douglas looked anywhere but at Luna, chain-smoking and sneering.

"Onward and upward, Larry. Let's see: 1988, kidnapping! Wow, big time, Lare." Luna clucked her tongue. "Charges dropped. But 1988 was a busy year. We got another rape charge, dropped, and an assault with a deadly weapon. Also dropped. And in 1989 you did another two in Huntsville for manslaughter. Released three months ago. Still on parole. Golly gee, Lare. This little stunt last night could get you right back there with extra

173

time." Luna leaned forward and said sweetly, "You call yourself a lawyer yet, hon?"

"Fuck you, bitch," Douglas responded.

"Now, Lare, there's a court-appointed attorney right outside, a Ms. Applegate, just dying to defend your sweet little ass."

"I don't want no cunt lawyer."

Luna clucked her tongue. "My, such language, Lare."

Luna moved so quickly I jumped. She lunged at Douglas, her face only inches from his. "Who paid you to off the Lesters? Who paid you to hit the house last night?" She knocked the cigarette from Douglas' mouth. "Who?"

"I didn't off nobody."

"Who?"

"I didn't kill nobody!" Douglas started to rise from his chair, but Luna knocked him back down.

"Who?"

"Swear to God I don't know shit about Lester. Whoever the hell he is. I just come along last night with Clyde, see. Me and Clyde were in the joint together. I seen him at Scooters yesterday and he says he got a job for me. Pay me five hundred bucks to go to this house and rough up some people. He didn't say nothing about offin' nobody. I swear to God."

Luna sat down in the chair opposite Larry Douglas. "You know something, sweet buns?" she said. "I believe you. 'Cause I don't think even Clyde'd be stupid enough to tell you anything important."

"Fuck you, bitch."

Luna laughed. "Jeez, with a vocabulary like that, maybe you should become a jailhouse lawyer, Lare. Whatcha think?"

She motioned with her thumb to the uniformed officer. "Get this scum back to his cell. And find somebody to represent him so we can send his ass back to prison."

Luna grinned at Douglas as he was ushered out of the room. "You ready to go back and take your butt fuckin' like a man, Lare?" she asked sweetly. He didn't answer.

# 17

We sat in the third booth on the left in Jolene's Cafe Dujour, Luna, Willis, and I, sipping lukewarm, mud-colored coffee, Luna and I eyeing the Danish under the fly-speckled glass dome on the counter.

"I know one thing Douglas lied about for sure," I said to Luna.

She took a sip of coffee and grimaced. "What's that?"

"His saying he didn't come to our house to kill any-body."

"What makes you say that?"

"Because," I sat up straight, the memory of my scene alone with Larry Douglas trying to bowl me over like a kick in the stomach, "when he had me alone, he said, and I quote, 'You're a hard bitch to kill'—kill being the operative word here."

Willis, sitting next to me in the booth, put his hand on my neck and kneaded the muscles. It felt good. Almost relaxing. My kids were safe at the police station. We were out in public with a cop and her gun. God's in His Heaven and all's right with the world. Sort of.

Luna shook her head, displacing my feeling of comfort. "Won't stand up in a court of law."

"What? The word of an upstanding citizen like myself against a creep like Larry Douglas?"

"Defense attorney would say it was a figure of speech, or you heard wrong, or he was just trying to scare you. Most rapists threaten their victims with death. If he goes down, and I'm pretty sure he will, it will be for attempted rape and breaking probation by associating with a known felon and carrying a gun."

"The son of a bitch tried to kill me and my kids!"

Luna motioned for me to keep my voice down. At this point, I really didn't care. "E.J., be prepared for the fact that the County Attorney's gonna try to bargain with both these guys—if Clyde ever comes out of it—to get the names of whoever paid them. Isn't that what you want? To get the person who's behind this? You don't think these guys were acting alone?"

I shook my head. "No, of course not. But I want them all. I want Clyde and Larry to get the death penalty and I want to be left alone for half an hour with whoever paid them."

Willis stopped kneading my neck and took a sip of coffee. "You don't believe in the death penalty," he said.

I gave him a dirty look. He shrugged. "Well, you've always said you didn't."

"Well, I don't . . . most of the time."

"Very convenient convictions you got there, babe," my husband of twelve years said.

"Can we drop politics for a moment and get back to reality?" I turned to Luna. "How is Clyde? Is he going to be able to talk anytime soon?"

Luna snorted. "His jaw's wired shut. He has a concussion, a lacerated left eye, had to have twelve stitches in

178

his forehead and three in his scalp, his nose is busted, and his left ear had to be partially sewn back on. But other than that . . .''

"What's wrong with his jaw?"

"You broke it."

"Oh." I thought for a moment, trying to keep out of my mind the fact that I, E. J. Pugh, had actually done that to another human being. Okay, so he was a human being trying to kill me and my kids, but still . . . "So how about we get a blackboard or something and go question him and let him write down his answers."

"If he's not illiterate," Luna replied.

"Well, we can try."

"What's this 'we' business, Pugh? Have I got a turd in my pocket?"

"What's that supposed to mean?"

"It's just an old saying."

I sighed heavily. "I know that! Jesus! I mean, you're not going to let us go with you? You let us watch you interview Douglas."

Willis grinned. "Or were you just trying to let us know what a truly ballsy broad you really are?"

Luna grinned back. "You mean there was ever a doubt?"

I allowed Willis one flirt a year. That was it and it was over as far as I was concerned. "We have a right, you know."

Luna looked at me and sighed. "Jeez, I don't know about ballsy, but you got the market cornered on pushy, Pugh."

I smiled. "Thank you. Shall we leave?"

We stopped by the station for Luna to pick up a small, lap-size blackboard and for Willis and me to check on the kids. Graham had Megan handcuffed to a table. Bessie was blithely coloring in her Sesame Street coloring book. We kissed them, said we'd be back soon, and left, going

179

out to Luna's unmarked patrol car and heading for Codderville Memorial Hospital.

Clyde Hayden was under guard on the top floor, the locked floor, of the hospital. A cop sat in a chair outside the door and another sat inside. The Codderville Police Department was finally paying some attention to what was going on around them.

He looked like shit. The guilt attack I got just looking at him could have felled a lesser woman. His head was swathed in bandages, as was his nose, his left ear, and his left eye. His jaw was indeed wired shut with a tube stuck in one side for breathing and another in the other side for liquids. An IV was plugged in one arm. His good eye looked at us as we came in, finally settling on me, where it stayed, following me as I moved around the room. It wasn't the most benevolent of eyes.

"Hey, Clyde, how you doing?" Luna greeted, sitting down in the chair next to his good side and patting his arm gently. "I'm Detective Luna and these are Mr. and Mrs. Pugh, the people you tried to kill."

A sound came out of his mouth but it was indistinguishable. Luna handed him the blackboard and some chalk. "Here you go, fella. Make life a little easier for you. Can you read and write?"

He gave her the look he'd been giving me and scratched out "eat shit and die" on the blackboard.

Luna smiled broadly at us. "Well, see now, I told you old Clyde wasn't an illiterate." Turning back to Hayden, she said, "Now, Clyde, honey, I want you to write down on that blackboard the name of the person who paid you and old Larry to off this nice family." She patted his arm again. "You gonna do that for me, darlin'?"

"Fuck you" was scratched on the board.

"Tsk, tsk," Luna said. "Such language. Well, I guess I'll tell the prosecutor to go ahead with the death penalty he's talking about for you two."

180

Clyde's eye got wide and he pointed at Willis and me. "Their alive!" he scratched.

Luna laughed. "You're right. They sure are." Pointing to the blackboard, she said, "And that should be *t-h-e-y* apostrophe *r-e*. It's a contraction. As in 'they are.' " Luna shook her head. "No, honey, I'm not talking about the death penalty for the Pughs. I'm talking about the Lester family. You remember? The mama and papa and the little boy you got on the stairs and that pretty little teenaged girl?"

Clyde shook his head so hard one of the bandages loosened. Luna reached up and stuck it, not so gently, back to Clyde's skin. "There you go. Now don't you go thrashing around like that. We want you nice and healthy for when the State sticks you with that old needle, now don't we?"

Frantically, Clyde scratched out "don't know no Lesters!!!!!"

"You don't? Well, maybe you didn't catch their names when you were doing them. It happens."

Clyde shook his head again. Frantically. "No! Didn't kill nobody!" he scratched.

Luna looked at Willis and me. "Well, you know, who-ever hired the hit on you may have have hired a separate team to hit the Lesters. But the bad thing is, whoever did, Clyde and Larry are going to go down for it." She shrugged and held up her hands in a helpless gesture. "We don't have any other names—"

The scratching sound of chalk on blackboard stopped Luna. She looked towards the board outstretched in Clyde's hands. "Billy Dave Petrie—Birdsong Road—out-side of Brenham".

Luna smiled and took the blackboard out of Clyde's hands. "Thanks, Clyde. We'll go talk to Billy Dave. You get well now, you hear?"

181

As we walked out, I turned towards Clyde. "Sorry," I said and shrugged. He didn't look pleased.

Back at the station, Luna got a book of maps and looked up Birdsong Road, looking in the general area of Brenham. She found it in Washington County, fifteen miles outside Brenham off Farm to Market Road 2340. Willis called his mother to come get the kids, telling her to take them to her sister's house in La Grange. We didn't want the kids anywhere our unknown mastermind could find them.

After finding out what we planned on, Luna called the La Grange Police Department, securing a patrolman to watch Aunt Louise's house. With that peace of mind, we got back in the city car and headed for Birdsong Road.

Brenham is the bluebonnet capital of Texas. It's also where the best ice cream in the world is made—Blue Bell. The road between Codderville and Brenham is a two-lane blacktop, and in mid-April, the roadside was covered with bluebonnets, Indian paintbrush, primroses, buttercups, and a thousand other varieties of wildflowers. They grew so heavily and so densely they touched the road, some blackened from bad exhaust systems. It took us forty-five minutes to find the sign saying Washington County, and another twenty minutes to find the mailbox on Birdsong Road that said "Petrie."

The mailbox itself should have told us something. The door to the box was hanging open from all the circulars and junk mail hanging out. We drove up the rutted, dirt drive, splashing mud on the clean city car from the puddles left by a recent rain.

Four vehicles sat in the yard of the dilapidated trailer house: a broken-down Ford pickup sitting on rims; a Chevy Malibu, not unlike Luna's own, three shades of brown, one being rust, its hood up and the motor on a hoist suspended from a tree above it; a three-wheeled motorcycle, the kind you see in the Hell's Angels movies;

and a brand-new Toyota four-by-four with gigantic tires, what a friend of mine refers to as a "Texas Clown Truck."

All this sat in front of a trailer any self-respecting tornado should have put out of its misery years ago. The front door of the trailer stood open, and as we got out of the car and walked towards the door, the odor almost knocked me over. Willis grabbed my arm and pulled me back. Luna said, "Shit," under her breath. Turning, she said to Willis, "You know how to work a two-way radio?" He nodded his head. "I think we're still in range. Get the station and have them call the Washington County sheriff's office. I need backup on this thing."

Willis ran to the car while I stood where I was, watching Luna pull a hanky out of her purse to cover her mouth, her gun ready in her right hand. With her foot, she opened the door wider and stepped inside.

# 18

It took less than five minutes for Luna to come out of the trailer. It took twenty for the Washington County sheriff's department to arrive. According to Luna, there were three bodies inside the house, those of two men and a woman. One of the men had ID that identified him as Billy Dave Petrie. The other one was somebody named Travis Munson. The woman was Beverly Munson. They'd all been dead for several days. All lying on their stomachs, hands tied behind their backs, bullet holes in their skulls. Execution style. The Mafia comes to Central Texas? Hardly, but the videotapes of the *Godfather* series are available almost anywhere.

Luna answered questions for another twenty minutes, then we left, getting back in the Codderville Police Department unmarked squad car and heading home. Having Luna drive us to Black Cat Ridge, we gathered the kittens and their paraphernalia, packed a suitcase for ourselves, and dropped the kittens off at the nearest boarding facility. Then Luna took us to a motel on the outskirts of town. It was a shabby place, its only saving grace being the dirty movies they piped in for their patrons.

"What now?" I asked Luna as she searched the small motel room for hordes of marauders.

"Ya got me by the ass," she replied, sticking her head out of the bathroom.

She came into the room and flopped down on the bed, shaking her head. "I'd say, offhand, we're at a standstill. Larry took us to Clyde, who took us to Billy Dave, who's not taking us anywhere. Unless the Washington County people find something incriminating in the trailer . . ." Her voice trailed off. "I'm getting fucking tired of unsolved mysteries," she said. "And this one's not even mine. I've got my own cases to worry about."

Willis sat down on the bed and began to massage her shoulders. I started to ask if they'd prefer to be alone. But I didn't. "What are you working on?" he asked.

Luna moaned and moved her head to get my husband's hands in a better position. I sat down in the only chair in the room and glared at them.

"'Member that school counselor, Mrs. Olson, who died in the car wreck last week?"

Willis said, "No, didn't hear about it."

"I did," I said. They both looked at me, as if surprised I was in the room. "I read about it in the paper."

Luna nodded. "Yeah, well, it wasn't an accident. Somebody cut her brake line." Luna shook herself, pulling away from Willis. "You keep that up and I'll go to sleep. And there's no rest for the wicked, as they say." She got up and moved to the door. "I'll send a squad car around to keep an eye on you two. Meanwhile—" she grinned and turned on the TV "—have a ball!"

She left and I glared at my husband. "What?" he said, all innocent.

"Hands that massage another shall never massage me, asshole," I said.

Willis laughed. "God, I love it when you turn that particular shade of green."

"Sitting there trying to turn that woman on!"

"I wasn't!" But he was still grinning.

"Making a fool out of yourself!"

"Me? I'm making a fool of myself?"

"Lying on a bed in a motel room with a woman you barely know!"

"*Sitting* on a bed in a motel room with a woman who's very tired and who's been through a lot."

"What am I? Chopped liver?"

He pulled me down on the bed. "You are most decidedly not chopped liver."

We stared at the picture on the TV screen. It was entirely too bizarre even to try to describe. Willis turned his head sideways, staring at the screen. Then the other way. Finally, he nibbled my ear. "You wanta try that?"

I pulled at his T-shirt. "Is our Blue Cross paid up?"

We were half undressed and pursuing a rather unusual line of foreplay when I sat bolt upright in the bed, knocking Willis to the floor.

"What the hell!" he said, rubbing his head.

"Mrs. Olson! She was Monique's sponsor in the PAL program!"

"What's that?" He crawled back up on the bed and began nibbling.

I pushed him away. "Peer Assistance and Leadership. The juniors and seniors counseled the freshman and sophomores."

"Okay. Now the big question: So?"

"So . . . I don't know! But there's got to be a connection. We thought all this time somebody was after Roy. But don't you see? It didn't have to be Roy. It could have been Terry, or Aldon . . . or Monique! Monique is murdered and then her counselor is murdered! That's a coincidence?"

Willis shrugged as he leaned towards my neck, his tongue searching out that particular spot. "Could be."

I jumped off the bed and pulled the sheet up to cover my body. It's not what it used to be, but Willis still seems to have a one-track mind when it's bared to him.

"I'm calling Luna!" I said, reaching for the phone.

Willis moaned. "Jesus H. Christ, Eej. Enough! We're in a motel room. The kids are fifty miles a way—safe. We've got a dirty movie on the TV. Relax, damn it!"

I picked up the phone and dialed Luna's home number, giving her the information I'd given Willis.

"Hum," she said.

"Hum? *Hum?* That's all you've got to say?"

"What? Okay, it's a coincidence!"

"Fuck coincidence!"

"E.J., such language."

"Don't try your perp rap on me, Luna!" I took a deep breath and plunged ahead. "All I'm saying is we may have been looking in the wrong place. It doesn't have to have been Roy who was the target. It could have been Monique."

"What? She and Mrs. Olson were running drugs through the school? Jesus, E.J."

"No! For Christ's sake. Luna, listen." To what, I didn't know. "Something they had in common. Something to do with the PAL program."

"What? Fourteen-year-old kids griping because their mothers make them take out the garbage? I've got one of those. Believe me, it's not worth killing people over."

"Check the school."

"I've checked the school. Fifty times. Everybody loved Mrs. Olson. Nobody wanted to off her."

"But you said somebody did."

There was a silence on the line. "E.J. Go screw your husband." She hung up. And I took her advice.

The next day we rescued our car from the police department parking lot and drove to La Grange to pick up the kids. I liked going to Aunt Louise's house because Aunt Louise liked me. Also because she baked. There were always fresh cookies, pies, and cakes at her house. Aunt Louise was four-foot-eleven and weighed one hundred and fifty-five pounds. But, God, could she bake.

We sat around in the old-fashioned living room, holding our china plates heaped with goodies, our linen napkins spread daintily on our laps, and talked. The kids were in the kitchen playing. Actually, Megan and Graham were arguing and Bessie was coloring.

"Well, goodness, I think you should all just stay here until they find these horrible people," Aunt Louise said.

"I got a home to take care of and dogs that need me," Mrs. Pugh said, her arms crossed over her chest, that "don't tread on me" look on her face.

"Now, Vera, you can take those dogs to the vet and board them. Or you can bring them here." The last was purely altruistic, as everyone knew Aunt Louise hated dogs.

"Nobody's after me," Mrs. Pugh said. "Willis and E.J. and the kids are the ones who need to hide out here. Not me."

"Well," Aunt Louise said, clearly giving in and thankful to do it, "Vera, if you think it will be safe . . ."

"Safe as houses," she declared, and got up to get her purse. "I'm driving back now, Willis. I want you to stay here with Aunt Louise until all this nonsense goes away."

"Yes, ma'am," Willis answered dutifully. He kissed her on the cheek.

Mrs. Pugh turned to me. "You okay?" she asked.

I smiled wanly. "I'm fine, Mrs. Pugh."

She looked at me a long time. Then she said, "Call me Vera." She grabbed her purse firmly in front of her. "Well. I'll be talking to you."

I almost choked on a rum ball. I glanced at my husband, who was grinning at me. "Welcome to the family," he said.

I went back to my plateful of rum balls and soda bread while Willis walked his mother to the car.

Aunt Louise was in the middle of a story about a friend of hers whose son was murdered by a guy wielding a hacksaw (it took a long time to do it, but the murderer persevered). I was only half-listening, the other part of my mind thinking how much Monique would have loved the story. Pretty, tiny Monique with her penchant for Freddy Krueger movies and heavy metal music. Monique, at sixteen a senior, a year younger than the others, trying so hard to be as adult, as silly, as cool as them. She was such a dichotomy of the teenager; silly and serious, childlike and grown-up. Would Megan and Bessie be like that when they were sixteen? Would they apply their mascara remembering exactly how Barbie dressed for the "big date"? Would they switch from MTV to the Disney Channel with such abandon? Would they hide their secrets with grown-up next-door neighbors?

I sat up straight on the horsehair sofa. My God, I thought. Oh, my God.

"What is it?" Willis asked, looking at me.

"We have to go home."

"Honey, we can't go home . . ."

I stood up. "Willis! We have to go! Now!"

I ran for the front door, turning to Aunt Louise. "You'll keep the kids?"

She was standing, her short, pudgy body all aquiver from the excitement she knew was there but didn't understand. "Of course!"

In my mind, as I ran for the car, I could hear Aunt Louise say, "Run! Run like the wind!"

I did.

# 19

We broke all the speeding laws and several other moving violations making the fifty miles from La Grange to Codderville in less than 45 minutes, with Willis bitching the entire way.

"We can't go back to the house!"

"We have to!"

"Why?" he demanded.

"Because I think there's something there that could . . . explain what's going on."

"Then let's stop right now and call Luna and have her meet us there."

"No! What if I'm wrong? I couldn't stand that again with Luna. She gets so uppity!"

"What do you think's there?" he asked.

I shook my head. "I don't know. Maybe nothing."

He hit the steering wheel with the heel of his hand. "E.J.!"

I sighed. "You know when I told you last year that

Monique was getting letters at our house from that boyfriend of hers that had joined the Marines?''

''Yeah, and I told you that was a total betrayal of your friendship with Terry and you said you'd tell Monique not to do it!''

''Well, I didn't have to. They broke up and the letters stopped.''

''Okay?'' He motioned with his hand for me to go on. And be quick about it.

''A few days before . . . before it happened, Monique brought me a manila envelope.''

''What?''

''She asked me not to look in it but to hide it.''

''Jesus, E.J.!''

''I thought it was boy stuff! I thought it was just Monique stuff! You know how dramatic she was! And it may be. I don't know. But, Willis, that school counselor . . .''

''Mrs. Olson.''

''Hurry.''

We shut up and Willis drove. He pulled up the driveway, stopping the car as close as possible to the back gate. He turned off the motor and we sat staring at our house, then both turning, as if our heads were attached to strings guided by an evil puppeteer, we looked at the house next door.

We got out and went in the back door of our house.

Standing in the kitchen, Willis said, ''Where is it?''

This was something I had been putting off since the thought had flashed through my mind. I didn't remember. ''I don't know,'' I said to Willis.

''What?''

''I can't remember!''

He shook my arm and I pulled away, glaring at him. ''I just can't remember! Jesus! Don't be so grabby!''

''When did she give it to you? Try to visualize it.''

192

"Try to visualize my fist up your butt!"

"E.J.!"

"Okay, okay. It was Friday afternoon. Terry was picking up the kids from school and Monique came home early. She came straight over here. She had this manila envelope. She asked me if I'd hide it for her like I had the letters last year. I told her I didn't want to get into that kind of thing again, but she said it wasn't like that. Then she asked me not to look inside, to please trust her, and I said of course I wouldn't look inside. And I didn't."

"What did you do with it?"

"I told you I don't remember!"

"Close your eyes. Okay, Monique's standing there. She hands you the envelope. It's in your hands. You walk with it . . ."

"I put it in the utility room!"

We both ran for the door of the utility room. There on the shelf above the detergents, bleaches, and fabric softeners was the envelope, sitting atop my box of rags. I reached up and pulled it down and opened it. Inside was the imitation leather diary with the faux gold lettering spelling out "Journal." I opened the front page. On it, in bright red Magic Marker, were the words, "PAL PROGRAM." Willis leaned over my shoulder and we both read.

Twenty minutes later we parked at the police station and rushed inside to Luna's desk.

"What now?" she asked, her eyebrow raised in that way she has of doing that I can't compete with. One eyebrow. I always wanted to do that.

I held out the journal. "Read this," I said. She took the book and read.

Ten minutes later, she looked up. "Jesus Christ."

Willis and I just stared at her. She turned to a uniform at the desk behind her. "Get me an arrest warrant. Make it out in the name of Berry Rush."

Willis and I waited until the warrant was issued, each of us sitting silently with our thoughts, while Luna busied herself making copies of the ledger. When the uniform brought the forms, Luna grabbed her purse and headed to her car. Willis and I were hot on her trail.

We found Berry Rush in his church office, being officious. He looked up quizzically as we burst into the room.

Luna slapped the warrant on his desktop. "Reverend Rush, you have the right to remain silent, you have the right to an attorney. If you cannot afford an attorney, one will be appointed to you—"

"What in the world?" He looked at Willis and me. "Willis, E.J., what is going on here?"

Luna finished reading him his rights. "Do you understand these rights as I have outlined them to you?"

"Of course, officer, I'm not an idiot. What in the world are you arresting me for, if I may be so bold?"

"For the murders of Roy Lester, Terry Lester, Monique Lester, and Aldon Lester."

Reverend Rush, who'd been lifting himself from his chair, sank back down. "My God."

"Do you wish to waive your right to an attorney?"

He shook his head, his hand reaching out for the phone. "May I call the church attorney now?" he asked.

Luna nodded and he picked up the phone.

We drove back to our house in Black Cat Ridge, calling Aunt Louise to let her know all was well and to ask if she'd keep the kids another night.

"Of course, honey. They're such a joy." She sighed. "I just can't believe it. A man of God! Doing such a thing."

"I know," I said. "It's unbelievable. But it's happened before."

I hung up and sat down on the couch with my husband, who was reading the copy of the journal Luna had given us. I read over his shoulder for what seemed the thousandth time. There was a lot to sink in.

*January 14—*

*Met with Eric Rush today. I feel so sorry for him. He doesn't have any friends, and all the girls treat him like a leper. If he'd do something about those zits it might help. But I think it's more than that. It's like he's got the weight of the world on his shoulders. We're meeting after school today at the Dairy Queen for a Coke. I just hope nobody thinks I'm dating him. Boy, is that an uncool thing to say, or what?*

*January 15—*

*I met with Eric at the Dairy Queen. He started crying right there and it was really embarrassing. Sometimes I think I'm not cut out for this counseling shit. Need to talk to Mrs. Olson about that. Anyway, we left the Dairy Queen and started walking. We took the trail by the railroad tracks and then walked down the tracks. He didn't say much but I think he's beginning to trust me because I don't let on how gross I think he is. But he's sweet, too, really.*

*January 18—*

*Spent my lunch hour with Eric today. Got him to smile. But that's about all.*

The journal went on in that vein until early March. That's when things began to get interesting.

*March 3—*

*Oh, God. Now what do I do? Met with Eric today. I never thought doing this PAL thing would lead to people telling me shit like he did! I've got to talk to Mrs. Olson. I'm also going to write all this down so I don't get any of my facts screwed up. This is sooooooo awful!!!!!*

*When they lived in Houston, before Eric's dad got our church here, Eric's sister got in trouble. Rev. Rush is always talking about how abortion is wrong and he*

wants the whole congregation to back him in that
Right to Life stuff. Nobody much listens to him at our
church, but it seems while they were in Houston, Rev.
Rush and Mrs. Rush were real big in the Right to Life
Movement there and had a lot of followers. Anyway,
when Eric's sister got knocked up, she was only sixteen
(and a preacher's daughter—but I've always heard
preacher's kids are the wildest!) and her parents took
her to Mexico for an abortion! Anyway, it got botched
up and they had to give her a hysterectomy. When they
came home, his sister just cried and cried. And she told
Eric what they'd done. When he confronted his parents,
they got really angry and told him it wasn't true. The
next day his sister was gone. He found out two years
later they'd put her in a mental institution! Can you
believe it! That poor kid's been holding this in all these
years! They threatened him once that he'd go there too
if he kept talking about "something that never
happened" so he hasn't mentioned it since. Except to
me. Oh, joy! I need Mrs. Olson's help on this one!

March 18—

I haven't seen Eric to talk to in two weeks, until
today. He's obviously been avoiding me. I told him I
had to go to Mrs. Olson with this. He got really upset. I
tried to calm him down but he just ran away. Now
what the hell do I do?

March 27—

Finally got up the nerve to speak to Mrs. Olson.
Haven't even seen Eric since the last time I talked to
him. Hasn't been in school. Mrs. Olson was very upset,
even though she tried to cover it up. She said for me to
forget about it and she'd take care of it. Thank God it's
off my shoulders.

March 31—

Eric's back in school. He came up to me at my locker

196

*and said for me to watch out. Said he'd told his*
*parents he told me! Gross! How can I ever go back to*
*church? He seemed really scared and it sorta scared me*
*a little. I'm going to hide these papers for*
*insurance—just call me Magnum, P.I.!!!!!*

That was Monique's last entry in her journal. Three days later she was dead.

Willis and I lay in bed together later that night, naked, our legs entwined, and I wondered if other people's sex lives perked up when their lives were in jeopardy. Terry would get a kick out of the whole thing. "Well, at least something good came out of this mess," she'd say.

Willis snored gently next to me. I closed my eyes and drifted, wondering who was smoking in my house. We didn't allow smoking in the house. I had a little sign in the living room, with daisies and mushrooms that said THANK YOU FOR NOT SMOKING. So why were they smoking in my house? Was it Roy? He quit. That's right. Roy wouldn't be smoking in my house. He quit.

I jerked myself awake, coughing. The house was on fire. I grabbed Willis and shook him. "Wake up!" I screamed. "We're on fire!" I grabbed the telephone next to the bed and dialed 911. Nothing happened. I depressed the button and listened. No dial tone. Willis was still out next to me. I hit him and hit him, finally kicking him to the floor where there was air to breathe. He woke up on impact, groggy but awake.

"The house is on fire!" I yelled.

He jerked upwards. "The kids!"

I grabbed him. "They're at your aunt's! Remember?"

He nodded and we crawled towards the window. We opened it and kicked out the screen, crawling onto the roof over the breakfast room. Smoke billowed out of our open window. We heard a crash from below and flames leaped out of the living room window.

197

Willis said, "I'll jump first then catch you."

"Oh, shit!"

"Honey, just do it!"

He jumped onto the grass in the back yard, landing hard on his left leg. Struggling, he stood up, holding out his hands for me.

"Jump, baby!" he yelled.

I looked at him and beyond. At Rosemary Rush coming up behind him with the five-gallon metal gasoline can. I'd barely begun to scream when she hit him on the back of the head.

# 20

Willis took the back scratcher and tried to edge it down inside the cast on his leg. "Fucking thing," he muttered.

I looked at the kids playing on the floor in the living room. "Language," I said, looking at my husband. At the rakish tilt of the bandage on his head, at the much autographed cast on his broken leg.

Rosemary Rush's aim was good—not fatal. Neither was my falling on her, though at the time I had murder on my mind. Willis was in the hospital for two days with a concussion and a broken leg from jumping off the roof. Our house was totaled. We were currently living in the Lester's house. I'd talked to Elaine about it and she said it would be okay for now. But maybe not as a permanent thing.

Berry Rush was out of jail. Rosemary was in. Berry's career was ruined, that was a sure thing, but after listening to Luna's account of Rosemary Rush's ramblings, it came out that Berry had known nothing about the murders. He'd been a prime mover and shaker in the institutionalization of his daughter. And for that I'd never forgive him. The girl, Ruth, had some problems but nothing that needed institutionalization. She was out now, over twenty-one and had been made responsible for her younger brother. They'd moved away, the two of them, and as I understand it, not even Berry knows where they are.

Rosemary told Luna that she had to do it. "Reverend Rush's career was in jeopardy," she'd told Luna. Which proved my theory right: even Rosemary called him "Reverend Rush." She'd hired Billy Dave Petrie to kill the Lesters and Mrs. Olson, and later, when Marilou Tanner had innocently let slip that I was calling to get the number of a private detective from her, she had instructed Petrie to kill Willis and me and the kids. He'd farmed out the Pugh family to Larry and Clyde, to our benefit. We might not have made it if Billy Dave had done this one himself.

He'd charged five hundred dollars for the Lesters and another five hundred for us. They came back, demanding more money. She said she'd meet him at his place with the ten thousand. The gun she used was one Reverend Rush kept in his sock drawer. The police found it, back snug with the socks, when they went through the parsonage with a search warrant. She said she was sorry about the young couple in Billy Dave's house.

"They shouldn't have been there," she told Luna. "But, they were trashy anyway." She wrinkled her nose and giggled. Girls will be girls, she seemed to be saying.

The will was through probate and we had access to the moneys left by the Lesters. I paid off the bills that had accumulated because of the funerals and had that off my chest. And we had the house. Our own insurance would cover the rebuilding of our home, eventually.

We'd been to see Elaine. All of us. Bessie saw her twice a week, once alone and once with Megan. Graham saw her once a week by himself. Willis and I saw her twice a week, once each separately and once for the whole family. The bills were getting outrageous, but we were beginning to learn to live with what had happened. And that's what mattered.

The First Methodist Church of Black Cat Ridge had a new minister, straight out of seminary. His name was Keith Reynolds and he wasn't nearly as bad as Berry Rush. Of course, he wasn't as good as Beth Asbury either. He was married, to a little girl named Robin, who giggled a lot. She dotted the *i* in her name with a happy face.

I sat in the living room watching the soap opera Willis had become addicted to since his stint at home. The kids played. A little too roughly, perhaps.

Megan grabbed Bessie and began to tickle her, rolling over on top of her. Bessie began to scream. ''Mommy! Mommy!''

I jumped up and ran to where the girls were. Megan had scooted away from Bessie, staring at her. Graham sat still, his eyes big as saucers. The kittens, Bert, Ernie, and Axl Rose, who'd been playing with the girls, all backed off to stare. Willis strained to get up.

Bessie threw her arms around my neck, her eyes squinched shut. ''Mommy, get off, get off!'' she cried.

I had a sudden vision. The killers in the hall upstairs. Shots ringing out. Aldon dead. Roy dead. Terry running to Bessie's room. Bessie's not there. She's sleeping with Monique again, the way she likes to do. Terry runs in there, screaming at Monique to wake up. The killers come up behind her. They shoot her in the back. Her body falls on the sleeping Bessie. Then they shoot the standing Monique, her body being flung against the back wall. And the killers leave. They don't know, or don't care, about the four-year-old trapped under her mother's dead weight. How long did she lie there? How hard did she have to fight to get out from under Terry? At what point did her mind just shut down?

"Mommy, wake up! Wake up, Mommy!" Bessie screamed.

I turned to Willis. "Call Elaine," I said.